PENGUIN B...
DYING AL...

Born in 1927 in western Punjab, now p... Vaid lived through harrowing expe... trains during the carnage that accomp... cites his transplantation, in 1947, to t... his most traumatic and central experience to date.

Vaid was educated at Punjab University (Lahore and Chandigarh) and Harvard University (Cambridge, Massachusetts), and has taught English and American literature at the Delhi and Punjab universities, and at three US institutions, Brandeis University (Waltham, Massachusetts), Case Western Reserve (Ohio) and the State University of New York.

He has published over twenty-five books in Hindi and English. His stories have been published in major Hindi and English magazines in India, and numerous foreign literary journals. Two of his novels (*Steps in Darkness* and *Bimal in Bog*), a short-story collection (*Silence*) and a book of literary criticism (*Technique in the Tales of Henry James*), were published in English to critical acclaim.

BY THE SAME AUTHOR:

In Hindi

Novels
Uss ka Bachpan
Bimal Urf Jayen to Jayen Kahan
Nasreen
Doosra Na Koi
Dard La Dava
Guzara hua Zamana
Kala Kolaj

Short Story Collections
Beech ka Darvaza
Mera Dushman
Doosre Kinare Se
Lapata
Uss ke Bayan
Meri Priya Kahanian (Selected Stories)
Voh aur Main
Khamoshi (Vol. 1 of Collected Stories)
Alaap (Vo1. 2 of Collected Stories)
Pratinidhi Kahanian (Selected Stories)

Translations from the English
Godot ke Intezaar Mein (Waiting for Godot)
Aakhiri Khel (Endgame)
Phaedra (Phaedre)
Alice Ajoobon ki Duniya Mein (Alice's Adventures in Wonderland)

In English

Translations from the Hindi of his own Work
Steps in Darkness (Uss ka Bachpan, a novel)
Bimal in Bog (Bimal Urf Jayen to Jayen Kahan, a novel)
Silence (Khamoshi, vol. 1 of collected short stories)

Translations from the Hindi of Others' Works
Days of Longing (Veh Din)
Bitter Sweet Desire (Doosri Baar)

Literary Criticism
Technique in the Tales of Henry James

Dying Alone
A NOVELLA
and
TEN SHORT STORIES

Krishna Baldev Vaid

PENGUIN BOOKS

Penguin Books India (P) Ltd., B4/246 Safdarjung Enclave, New Delhi 110 029, India
Penguin Books Ltd., 27 Wrights Lane, London W8 5TZ, UK
Penguin Books USA Inc., 375 Hudson Street, New York, New York 10014, USA
Penguin Books Australia Ltd., Ringwood, Victoria, Australia
Penguin Books Canada Ltd., 10 Alcorn Avenue, Suite 300, Toronto, Ontario M4V 3B2, Canada
Penguin Books (NZ) Ltd., 182-190 Wairau Road, Auckland 10, New Zealand

First published in English by Penguin Books India (P) Ltd. 1992

Copyright © Krishna Baldev Vaid 1992

All rights reserved

The English translations in this book previously appeared as follows: *Dying Alone*, excerpts in *Debonair* (February 1992) and *Bombay Literary Review* (1991, No. 1); 'Silence', in *Botteghe Oscure* (Number XXV, 1960) and *Silence and Other Stories* (Writers' Workshop, Calcutta, 1972); 'The Stone of a Jamun', in *Weber Studies* (Vol. 7, No. 2, Fall 1960); 'The Voice-Robber', in *The Times of India* (13 September, 1991); 'My Effigy', in *The Times of India* (6 February, 1991); and 'The Soul of Darkness', in *The Times of India* (26 June, 1991).

The stories in this book originally appeared in the Hindi as follows: *Dying Alone*, as *Doosra Na Koi*, a novella, by Parichaya Prakashan, Hapur (1978); 'Silence', as '*Khamoshi*', in *Beech ka Darvaza*, a short-story collection, by Neelabh, Allahabad (1963); 'The Stone of a Jamun', as '*Jamun ki Guthli*', in *Beech ka Darvaza*, a short-story collection, by Neelabh, Allahabad (1963); 'The Voice-Robber', as '*Avaz Chor*', in *Saptahik Hindustan* (15 October, 1989); 'My Effigy', as '*Putla*', in *Sarika* (December 1989); 'The Soul of Darkness', as '*Andhere ki Atma*', in *Saptahik Hindustan*, (15 October, 1989); 'The Fourth Window', as '*Chowthi Khirki*', in *Sarika Times* (15 November, 1990); 'The Thieves' Thief', as '*Choron ka Chor*', in *Sakshatkar* (April-June 1990); 'An Evensong', as '*Shaam*', in *Sarika* (January 1990); and 'An Evening with Bhookh Kumari', as '*Bhookh Kumari ke saath Ek Shaam*', in *Saptahik Hindustan* (11 August, 1990). Sections I, II, III, IV, VI and VII of 'The Old Man in the Park' appeared as '*Saye*', in *Dharmayug* (17 December, 1989); section V appeared as '*Aage Dekho Fatehpuri*', in *Samkaleeen Bharatiya Sahitya* (July-September 1990); and section VIII as '*Antim Sair*', in *Indraprastha Bharati* (April-June 1990).

Typeset in Palatino by Digital Technologies and Printing Solutions, New Delhi
Made in India by Ananda Offset Private Ltd., Calcutta

This book is sold subject to the condition that it shall not, by way of trade or otherwise, be lent, hired out, or otherwise circulated without the publisher's prior written consent in any form of binding or cover other than that in which it is published and without a similar condition including this condition being imposed on the subsequent purchaser and without limiting the rights under copyright reserved above, no part of this publication may be reproduced, stored in or introduced into a retrieval system, or transmitted in any form or by any means (electronic, mechanical, photocopying, recording or otherwise), without the prior written permission of both the copyright owner and the above mentioned publisher of this book.

for Champa

Contents

Dying Alone (a novella)   1

Short Stories   107

   Silence   109

   The Stone of a Jamun   120

   The Voice-Robber   134

   My Effigy   137

   The Soul of Darkness   139

   The Fourth Window   141

   The Thieves' Thief   145

   An Evensong   149

   An Evening with Bhookh Kumari   153

   The Old Man in the Park   168

Dying Alone
a novella

One

My house looks like a bloated monster. About to die. Or perhaps about to to be resurrected.

I came up with this strained simile after a considerable effort. I had to get up and pace the floor and sit down and pant several times. When I still had hair I could get out of my blocks sometimes by rubbing my head instead of having to get up and pace. When my hair began to fall like autumn leaves I had to pull out the ones that were left in order to arrive at my analogies. Now my skull is absolutely bare. If I happen to run my hand over it I feel as if I am a blind old woman asking a soggy papaya: Are you sweet? I am grateful that my nails now are as limp as my flesh. Even if I happen to scratch my skull I don't quite scratch it. In other words my skull has become immune to caresses and curses. Of course, even now, every now and then, it comes suddenly alive with strange sensations. And I can't but marvel at the mischievous mysteries of Nature.

Just now I have an urge to break this pen and tear this notebook to pieces; before starting to squeeze my soggy skull. Until it bursts like a ripe boil. And my fingers are drenched in the goo or pus or whatever it is that fills it. And my notebook is besmeared with yellow and red stains. I am held back by the fear that nothing but foul air will come out of it.

Even pacing doesn't produce the result it used to. The moment I decide to get up and pace, my hands get up and perch on my knees. Like two famished birds. And a deadly smile comes and sits down on my lips. Like a wasp. And I drop my decision. And I begin to wish I could change into a statue or a saint. So that the desire to get up and pace or probe into the puerilities of my self is destroyed. But whenever I am blocked I have to do something. No matter whether I can or not. I often suggest to myself that I should have cultivated a trick more original than pacing the floor. Then I suggest to myself that no trick is altogether original.

I knew the above para would end on the sentence it did. I knew it but couldn't do anything about it. Because my weakness for pseudo-philosophy hasn't died yet. No weakness ever dies before one's death.

Of late, instead of pacing, I have started regressing to another ruse in order to remove my blocks. That too is not very original. But it does excite me all the same sometimes. When it becomes imperative and impossible to straighten out an awkward analogy or caress a sulky sentence or rid a period of its pride—I haven't been able to discard my habit of saying the same thing in at least three different and defective ways; will I ever?—instead of scratching my skull or dragging my feet about I let my hand loose in my private jungle. It is not much of a jungle now and my hand gets no immediate rise out of it. But as my fingers play with the undergrowth I sometimes sense a surprise in that neglected area. More frequently, however, I am reminded that my pubic region has become as soggy as my skull, that soon it will become as bare too, that soon my limp lord will look as bald as my head. These reminders always succeed in amusing me a little.

This house looks like a bloated monster. I have been dying in it for decades. Alone and disgruntled. In this unlively alien town. Where many others, equally or even more alone and disgruntled, have also been dying for decades. In their houses. To them, too, perhaps, their houses look like bloated monsters. But then not every dying person can come up with analogies like mine. But why not? I knew I wouldn't let myself go further without disputing this point. Perhaps all others too are sitting behind their windows, thinking these very thoughts, even writing them down, whenever the folly takes them, but I don't think so. There is a grave difference between them and me. They were born and raised in the snow and rain of this town, while I was not. I don't belong here. I belong nowhere now. There was a time when this used to overwhelm me. Now all I feel is a slight sinking of the heart and a faint tremor of the lips. The slight sinking of the heart perhaps signifies that the thought of belonging nowhere now produces a reaction of slight self-pity. But the tremor of the lips bears witness to a contradictory truth. My lips tremble as ever only in irony.

The above para barely saved itself from banality. Because of the reference to the lips. It began with short and breathless sentences, perhaps because I myself was breathless then. I can't count on my wind any more. It rises and subsides at will. The tone and the length of my sentences vary with my wind.

This house looks like a bloated monster. That I've been dying alone in it for decades is not unusual in this place. Everybody my age dies alone here. Like the old woman next door. The exquisite old woman next door. She is senior to me in age and shorter in size. According to the custom of this place I should know next to nothing about her even though she lives next door. She is dying in her house, I in mine. A few years before, I'd have automatically added to this sentence: If this can be called a house, if this can be called dying. For years we haven't seen each other. We step out of our houses at different times. She goes out at noon—for a walk, or on an errand. Or to a rendezvous. Or for nothing. Who knows! Who cares! At noon I am almost always sitting at this window, gorging myself upon my regrets. I leave my house late at night when she is dead asleep. So I shouldn't know much about her. But I do. This is how: three windows of the upper storey of my house open on the three windows of her single storey house, in such a way that, unless her blinds are down and curtains drawn, I can see everything in her house. Or at least enough to give me the gloomy illusion of having seen everything. When I am able to do nothing else, I peep into her daily life, or death, through my three windows. If her curtains are drawn and the blinds down, I wait till they are eventually undrawn and up. If I get tired, I fall to my knees. Sometimes I have to spend several days in this posture before my luck turns. For all I know, she too peeps into my daily life, or death, secretly. We have never caught each other actually peeping into each other's lives or deaths. Perhaps she is blind; has become blind, that is. I better avoid these casual conjectures about her or else I'll lose all interest in fabricating her story. But I have to record one more detail clearly about her for my own clarity. To me she looks much older than, in fact twice or even thrice as old as, I am. Old enough to be my mother or even grandmother. Paternal or maternal. Which is not to deny that, to me, I look old enough to be her older brother or her ancient lover. If not her father or her grandfather. An impartial observer might be able to tell who is actually older. But I have no intention of dragging in that hypothetical monster into all this.

Perhaps I should ask myself why I have dragged in the old woman into all this. Well, I am asking. The answer I get is why not! I am never surprised by any of my answers to any of my questions. At my age only bastards desire surprises. I should stop right here. There is no fun any more in flogging every dead sentence. There never was any. I have stopped.

I shouldn't have let the old woman enter so soon. But why not? She is as important to me as this monster of a house. It is not an apt analogy. This house is made of mud and wood. A lifeless monster. I am dying in it. If this endless living can be called dying. The old woman is made of old bones and sallow flesh. Short but lively. No bigger than a bird but lively.

My fingers had become woodstiff with writing so I decided to get up and gad about a little. I gave a new disorder to the disorder of this room. I kicked some of the things, and was kicked, in return, by some of them. Once or twice it seemed I had almost broken my knees and ankles. But my bones are unbreakable. Or I wouldn't have been here now making all this up. So many of my contemporaries are no more. I feel superior to them. In a sick sort of way. I can hear the snores of my sleeping guilt. My bones may be unbreakable but I am not. I shouldn't have gotten up. I am all numb with fatigue. I feel no pain anywhere. No this is not the numbness before the end. I will not end before my old woman. This resolution has stretched a dry and soundless laughter over my face. Like a transparent mask. It will take me quite a while to rip it off.

I must have come into this monster of a house centuries ago. It seems I have died numerous deaths since then. But the memories of my life before I came here are still alive and around. Like old dogs with their odours. There was a time when I used to mistake the stink for fragrance. Dogs do not have long lives. I shouldn't have compared my memories to dogs.

I shall compare this house to a bloated monster no more. A house is a house and a monster a monster. In my youth I would never have allowed an inane sentence like this to stand. Even in my youth I must have perpetrated many sentences even more inane than this. I can, if I like, compare myself to a shrivelled old monster. But I am only a shrivelled man. The occupant of this huge and unexciting house. Where I have been consuming my endless old age. I still indulge in self-pity but the habit has lost some of its old horror. The paint of this house has been peeling off ever since I came into it, but the wood underneath is as sound as my bones. I remember how years ago I used to scrape the paint off the porch with my nails. I used to sit every day all day on the porch. My nails still functioned like nails. Some sympathetic passers-by would stop and ask: So you are painting your palace, are you? I never bothered to tell them I was not painting. They must have known. They wanted to humour me. I let them. I wanted to discourage any further conversation. Sociable and sympathetic souls have always been insufferable to me. I can't brook being talked to by friendly strangers or even acquaintances. I claim, with pride, that I have never, in all my lives, initiated any conversation, never been the first to ask anyone about their spouses and children, or to comment on the cursed weather, or to moan or moon about life or the world in general. On the contrary, I've always responded to most such advances with fat frowns. When I was still in the world of ordinary affairs I was occasionally incensed by the thought that the others perhaps considered me a misanthrope. I was always comforted by the thought that I baited myself as much as I did others. My habit of self-pity notwithstanding.

To continue with the story, one day the old woman saw me standing on my toes trying to reach an unreachable spot on my porch. She asked in her crow's voice—What is it that you keep doing these days? Her neck those days used to stretch or shrink in accordance with the length of her sentences. I responded to her question by opening my claws quietly. She perhaps thought I was attempting an obscene gesture. She started laughing like a fat hen. I should have lost my temper. Normally I can't tolerate any outburst except my own. But there must have been something about the naked laughter of the old woman because I turned toward her and started laughing almost exactly like her. No, my laughter couldn't have been even remotely like hers. My laughter is incomparable. Perhaps it has some resemblance to the fluttering of an empty pocket. There she was, rocking in her chair on her porch, cackling away like a deaf mute at a foreign flasher. And here I was, standing on my porch, braying away like a dumb ass at a full moon. My eyes, I noticed, were drawn to her vibrant bosom. I wondered how they could be. At my age? At her age? With this thought my laughter took a different sound. I removed her dress from her quivering thighs and had a glimpse of her sagging flesh and grey bush. I was hoping to be revolted by the sight. On the contrary I felt a slight sensation in the dead spider suspended between my legs. I wondered how I could. At my age? At her age? A man and a horse never say die before death. I drew some strength from this silly saying. I saw her suddenly transformed into an ageless sorceress. An embodiment of an invitation to rise above my age. It was then that I realized that at my age no woman of any age less than hers would ever laugh like that at anything I did or said. Her bosom danced to her laughter.

I have noticed that some old women retain their bounce until the end. Is this rusty piece of observation all I have to show for all my experiences? I am suddenly bored with this memory. I must stop or I will have to dash my head against the floor again. The floor is wooden. Otherwise I would have split my head long ago. I will have to threaten myself with something else. In order to stop. I must stop or I will start breaking things. This too won't work. All things in this house are already broken. I don't have the strength to break them any further. A stranger would think this house is occupied by a beast, or a maniac, or a monster, or perhaps by all three.

A moment ago I was seized by the desire to spit in the direction of the old woman's house. I did so without getting the relief I had expected. I am a foolish old man. That is why I am in this condition or chaos or whatever it is. I am approaching my end, but continue to think in the same stupid way I used to when I wasn't even dimly aware of the end.

The old woman refuses to get out of my mind. Every day I think at least a couple of times that if I had gotten married to her I might have been freer of her now. But, then, I wouldn't have been freer of some other phantoms. Not that I am free of those other phantoms now. Not that I mind being haunted by the old woman. At this extremity nothing but this extremity can really bother me. I hear a voice that says this is not an extremity, even this doesn't really bother you. And I had begun to hope that I had finally lost this voice. No voice is wholly lost it seems. I knew I would not be able to suppress this sentence. If I had married the old woman I might have had to give up this house. Perhaps that was what saved her. It was she who proposed. This memory makes me feel an inch taller even now. Had I accepted her proposal she would have insisted on my move to her house. Her house is better than mine. Outside as well as inside. Perhaps her main motive in proposing to me was to get me out of this big, ugly house and into hers. Had I accepted her proposal and moved into her house, and sold mine to someone else and that someone else had demolished it and put up a beautiful house in its place, she might have divorced me and married him. Or lorded it over me with an iron will. And I would've started longing for my lost freedom. At my age one doesn't long for anything. At least I don't want to admit one does. I can't see myself dying in another house. When she proposed I was in her house, in her bed, anticipating her proposal. Perhaps she had insisted on my going to her house that night for that very reason. She might have thought it was necessary to lure me out of my lair in order to conquer me. That was the first night she had broken the rule and refused to come over to my house. Her excuse was her aching back. I had smiled, for, in the light of her aching back, my relationship with her looked suddenly ridiculous. I felt like telling her on the phone that I had had enough of her. But I pretended to be concerned. She claimed the ache in her back had been caused by my bed. I know my bed is not made of roses. It sags incredibly even under my little weight. Whenever she was with me in the bed our backs used to scrape against the floor through the mattress and springs. She is quite weighty. Perhaps that was why I fell for her. I have always fallen for fat women. I doubt if I shall ever cease to fall for them before the end. She threatened to hang up on me and said—Well, if you refuse to come over for once to my clean and beautiful bed, I am through with you. Good Night! I forgot to retort as I waited for the final click, but she went on to demand—Well, aren't you going to say yes or no; silence may be the custom of your country but I have to have an audible answer. I could never tolerate any insinuation of hers about my country. She knew my weak nerve. I shouted—What was that nonsense about my country? I could see her heaving with satisfaction and hugging the receiver to her billowy bosom. So I repeated in a cracked voice—What was that nonsense about my country? She started to laugh with her characteristic coarseness, and I to tremble with my characteristic impotence.

I want to stop here and observe a moment of silence for my country. I have done it.

Then she spoke, obviously through a mouthful of smoke—All I said was that you have to give me a straight answer, yes or no.

Those were the days when we used to have long and senseless talks on the phone. No one else ever called me even though I lived in constant hope of an unexpected call—of a call, in fact, to end all calls. I'm telling an unnecessary lie. I never hoped for any call to end all calls. In truth, long before I came to be entangled with her, I had given up waiting for the phone to ring. The phone sat in its corner like a dead black cat while I growled like an idle lion all over the house. My growl expressed more grief than anger. Now it expresses neither grief nor anger. Now it is no more than the receding echo of an old occupation. That is why it has been replaced by this record. Alas!

But I had had the phone installed, before assuming this house arrest, so as to remain in touch with the outside world—hospital, police, fire brigade, liquor shop, supermarket etc. Of course, at that time, I had no contact with the old woman or with anyone else, man or woman, young or old. The house arrest meant I had withdrawn from all contacts and turned my face to freedom—I mean, salvation. It was my kind of withdrawal from the world. Like donning the ochre robe without actually donning it. And, but for that infatuation at first sight with the old woman that fateful day on the porch, I would not have ended my withdrawal and gone back to the blasted world as it were. Alas!

I should beware of this alas, lest I should slip back into my old long-discarded style.

I was a little riled by the ultimatum in her voice. Yes or no, she had demanded. Had I said no, the affair would have ended right there. I had never before heard that note of peremptory precision in her voice. I felt as if miraculously she had recovered all of her long-lost teeth. I had gotten used to her fat sallow flesh. I have always been an abject creature of all my habits. Going over to her house would mean defying one of them. Until that night whatever had or had not happened, had happened in my bed, or around it. Now, had I not been scared by her ultimatum, I would have tried to destroy her by irony without any fear of being caught in the act. I would have said—Look, dear, I'll come over if you insist, but why don't you tell me first why you are so insistent on breaking the rule today? I mean, but for my fear of losing her altogether, I would have argued with her, and finally either won her over to my house or persuaded her to skip that night. Perhaps then she would have proposed to me on the phone. Perhaps we would have broken with each other. But all I did was to finally say in a feeble voice—Yes.

And, that night, a little later, as I lay next to her, naked and unarmed, amusing my body and mind with her billowy bosom, forgetful of the fact that I was in her house, in her bed, out of my own lair, she ignored my unstraight arrow and asked in an unfamiliar voice—Have you ever thought of marriage? Her question touched me like a red-hot rod. I discontinued whatever I was doing, or being done to, and burst out laughing while she stared at me like a bloated sow.

I am a foolish old man. Otherwise, instead of wasting my mind and memory, at my age, over this alien idiotic old woman, I would have been, like every other ordinary and insatiable old man, thinking of some crisp and unsoiled virgin, some youthful dolly, in order to arouse my dead rat. I haven't yet become so foolish as to waste all my mind over my one memory. I had better not disturb the swarm of memories from 'over there' or else I'll be beset with all those regrets and anxieties which I keep hidden under huge rocks, and which crawl all over me every night. Every night.

But I must carry on. In spite of, or rather, along with, that laughter, I was going insane with the sour and aged odour coming from her

Dying Alone

bed and body and from between my own legs. It seemed I was standing near an open sewer. Her bosom looked like two plastic bags full of fat. The blue veins on her calves and thighs, her rubbery lips, her harsh tongue hanging out of her mouth—she looked like a strange animal sitting on my nerves. My laughter was beginning to change into nausea. After staring at me a while she sat up and started to mutter. Now her boobs seemed to be talking to her knees. To her my own prostrate body must have looked like that of a dehydrated old child's. Somehow my laughter didn't quite soar into horror, nor did my nausea flow out of my nose. The old woman started to get out of the bed, cursing, and I continued to lie there, snickering, as if I wasn't worried about the end of our affair, as if there had been no reduction in the surprise, amusement, and disgust produced in me by her proposal. If she hadn't been selfish and stubborn, she would have continued to sit by me, or lie next to me, or fall all over me in an effort to revive my limp lord. And I would have closed my eyes and played with her balloons while waiting for my flower to bloom. And after a while she would have exclaimed—This is a case for Christ! She is very religious. I would have burst into yet another fit of laughter. And detecting a sensation in my soldier or devil or flower—all meaty metaphors are mixed—she would have started shoving it desperately into her dry well. I never helped her in that joyless and tortuous procedure. She often complained—If you stop acting like an indifferent observer, maybe we will get some pleasure out of this stupid act. She would never admit that, at our age, we could get no pleasure out of any pain. I am sure her culture and conditioning did not permit her to admit this. In any case I would have continued to squeeze her boobs with a cynical concentration. She often got angry at my ardour and said—I don't see what pleasure you derive out of kneading these dead dugs! I derived no pleasure. I always withdrew my withered root from her hand or hole or mouth and retorted—The same as you do from your efforts to arouse this dead beast or from stuffing it into your trough! She laughed at that like a fat hen. She often surprised me with her sense of humour.

But, on that momentous night, she didn't join me in my laughter. I had never even dreamt she would ever propose to me.

Had she not waddled into another room, after yet another long and scornful look at me, I might have tried to amuse her with my antics and make her see the ridiculousness of it all; I might have drawn her attention to my shrivelled body and asked—You mean, at your age, you want to marry this! I might have tickled my fool and said—Shouldn't you have consulted him first? But this old woman is too much. It is not inconceivable that she might have started singing a panegyric to me and my fool or delivering a tirade against my pessimistic outlook. She had a way with words. Perhaps I should have accepted her proposal. Then, instead of recording all this now, I would have been having royal rows with her, or pulling her boobs while she played with my poor bastard. Perhaps, even now, it is not too late. Perhaps I should pick up the phone as soon as the impulse unmans me someday and say—Look, old woman, after a lot of serious afterthought I've concluded I can't do without you; so let's get married so that you can resume your bouts with my brown banana.

I am a lecherous old man. I should thank God I can't stir out of this house any more. I would be arrested every time for teasing innocent old women. I should also thank all those other constraints because of which I cannot be my lecherous self. I'll list them a little later. If I am ever able to get rid of her and move ahead. I had never thought she'd hog my memoirs even after the end of our affair. I have already finished and torn several notebooks. I am not sure whether I'll be able to go through with this one. I had never thought she would usurp my attention to the extent she obviously has. But why grumble! She helps me to pass the time by helping me to blacken these blank pages. Of course we speak different languages. Metaphorically as well as otherwise. Perhaps it is my language that has prevented me from losing my past here. Not perhaps; certainly, perhaps. I don't have to be particular about precision at my age. I should say the first thing that rises to my lips, write the first word that descends on my pen, think the first thought that assaults my mind, and so on. I feel breathless. Because of this notion perhaps. I'll stop a while and take a few deep breaths. Just as I used to do

Dying Alone

when I was young. Every time I recall my raw youth, I appreciate this ripe age all the more. I'll explain this enigma later. Perhaps. No, positively. Perhaps.

But now, even if I do pick up the phone and offer myself, she won't accept me. I have lost count of the days or months or years that have gone by since that fateful night. She must have become oblivious of me by now. She may have even gone beyond my pale. Perhaps she won't hear me even if I howl. If I could still shed tears, I would have at this moment. For a while. Quite often I strip myself bare—I mean I take off my long shirt, which is all I wear—and stand patiently behind the window that opens on her boudoir. *Boudoir*! I hear a new sound in every archaic word. This too seems to be due to my distance from there. Perhaps I'll breathe my last luxuriating in the new sound of a long-forgotten word or metaphor. I should feel happy at the thought of my last breath. But like every other ordinary man I dread it, which is why I keep myself preoccupied by this old woman or this house or this condition or chaos or whatever it is or with my memories of there, trying in vain to arouse the vain rage I used to feel when I was young. I mean when I was less old, much less old. But now, at my age, I can't possibly move my rocks at will. I don't know what I mean by this coinage.

When the old woman returned from the other room, fully dressed, I was still lying in her bed, undressed, wondering at her proposal, laughing, feeling sick. While she was gone, I had put my dentures back in my mouth, but not quite properly, or perhaps her tongue-twisting kisses had made my gums mushy. I could feel the inside of my mouth aching softly all over, reminding me of the future without that soft ache, without her sallow flesh, without her billowy bosom. She stood beside the bed like a shapeless statue. From where I lay she looked taller than she was. Her eyes were narrowed as if she was threading a needle, or gazing at a tiny object with her weak vision, or trying to take a thorn out of somebody's sole. My hands were interlocked at my chest. This often gives my lungs and soul an unaccountable comfort. For a spell we remained silent. Then she beckoned me with her imperative finger to get the hell out of her bed. I just lay there. Like a spoilt child. She kept on giving me her imperious index finger. I closed my eyes and imagined that, if instead of that sallow alien old woman a dark young woman of my own kind had been standing beside my bed, giving me her imperious index finger, my foolish cock would have stretched its neck and started to crow. I imagined my mindless body lying under that of a tight mindless woman from the hills; I felt her greedy tongue exploring my ruined mouth, her grape-like fingertips rolling all over my sagging flesh and sere bones, her blind bosom-buds pressed against the grey-haired hollow of my chest, her naughty buttocks blossoming under my knotty fingers, her juice irrigating my fallow field, rejuvenating my poor farmer. I would have continued to keep my eyes closed forever, watching those various wonders, but a bat flew out of somewhere and clamped on the drunken lout between my legs, and I opened my eyes in horror. My mouth, always ajar, also flew wide open. The old woman was bending over me, with her arthritic claw on my sleeping lion, trying desperately to close it—her claw—into a fist. I feared she would break into two at the waist. She had suffered from backache for the past half century. Or so she claimed.

My fantasies had been devoured by the sallow reality bending over me and I reduced once again to an exhausted lecher at the behest of a bosomy old woman who was trying to arouse me or pull me by my root out of her bed. She must have misunderstood the untimely crispness of my normally limp lotus. She hissed through her clenched teeth—Get up or I'll pull it out! I felt her fist getting firmer and decided to submit. Slipping out of her hand, I started to get up to the tune of *Hé Rama*! The old woman couldn't stand my *Hé Rama*! I used to tell her I couldn't possibly rid myself of all the relics of my past, that, for me, *Hé Rama* was as indispensable as the last cry of Jesus for her. But she was not impressed by my analogies, nor softened by my torments. She maintained I was trying to con her by my *Hé Rama*! She had no interest in my glorious country or my grim past, nor did she have any knowledge of either. As she saw me getting up, she released me and withdrew her hand and started straightening herself, groaning loudly all the while. I could hear her bones crackling under the layers of her loose flesh. She would have heard mine had she not been deafer than I. I shouted as I put on my shirt—So you are kicking me out, are you? This was more of a last appeal than a simple question. She considered it for a second, then turned it down.

But why am I giving this incident the treatment of a touching story? To pass the time perhaps. This sentence stinks. It keeps rising to my pen. Even as it does to the lips and pens of millions of other miserable fools! I am trying to whip myself into a reaction or rage. It doesn't behove a man of my age to grumble. About anything. Particularly about time and stink. Nothing becomes a man of my age. Certainly not sentimentality. I don't care about what becomes me or doesn't, whether anything becomes me or doesn't. Fuck sentimentality. Fuck old age too. This imperative too has lost its fury. Perhaps it never had any. And there was a time when I used to crown every other sentence with it. It sounded not only effective but also funny then. It doesn't any more. Am I being nostalgic? Am I perhaps unwittingly missing my fucking friends? Many of whom preferred foul language. On principle. Because it was the language of the toiling masses. Am I perhaps unwittingly being sarcastic? Where are those friends now! Many of them must have passed on. Others must be in the process of doing so. Like me. I never had too many friends. Thank God! I do not remember their names. I remember their faces, faintly. Whenever I try to visualize them, I can't decide whether I should see them as I used to or as they must be now. It is just as well. Because I know I won't be able to see them more than faintly. Of course, sometimes, without any effort, in the course of a sleepless night or a nightmare, I do see some of them, but the faces they show are better forgotten. Which is why I can't forget them. Which is why I don't want to write about them. Which is why I am writing about them. Will I please cut it out? The voices of a couple of my long-lost friends do sometimes pierce my ears, even though I can't be sure that they are actually theirs, that they aren't really mine. I can't be sure they aren't emanations of my own undestroyed memory. I can't be sure of anything. Which doesn't entitle me to shouting. Quite suddenly I am sick of all this. If I could get up I would have gotten up, picked up some broken object, and smashed it against the window of the old woman's boudoir, or picked up the phone and shouted—What are you doing now, you old whore? And before she had recovered from the shock, I would have hung up, and waited for her to return my call.

I have taken a few sips of water and swallowed a pill. I have little pitchers of water lying all over this place so that one of them should always be within my reach in my dire need or whenever my throat should go dry. But this arrangement often results in my reaching for a liquid that is barely distinguishable in appearance and taste from my own water. The water in the pitcher I sipped from tasted different though. Perhaps I should spill it. But I won't. It doesn't really matter how it smells or tastes, as long as it is water. It can't be mine because I don't preserve mine. Also because I don't make enough to preserve. Because I don't drink enough to make enough. Which is why, perhaps, I have gout. In addition, of course, to numerous other ailments of which I am barely aware. Which is why, scattered all over the place, I have pills that are barely distinguishable in appearance and taste from my own droppings. Which is why I often mistake a dropping for a pill and vice versa. It is always too late for me to do anything about it. The water and the pill I swallowed a while before may have reduced my inertia a little, but haven't done a thing to my irritation. But, perhaps, irritation is necessary for my survival. But for it I would. . . . This sentence doesn't need an end. I may or may not need one but I can't be far from it. Hope springs eternal even in the most arid of minds. Ever since the end of my parents I have been freed of the dread of death. And of the memories and nightmares of that dear dreadful place. It seems they died centuries ago. But every day I manage to remember them under one pretext or another. No one will remember me after I am gone. This thought gives me a terrifying satisfaction. Whether I admit it or not, I still feel guilty about my parents. But, at my age, no guilt can give me the anguish I need. Or the anguish I used to experience some centuries ago. When every night was a nightmare. Now I only feel a fleeting twinge. As I am doing right now. But I can cope with it quite easily. But then can't I do so with everything now? This tired tone is due to the twinge I felt just now. Normally I am quite crisp. Too much of crispness too isn't good. The variation of tone is essential to the variation in the pace of time, which is essential for enduring, for continuing to endure, my anguish.

By calling this anguish anguish I am not really elevating it. I am only ridiculing it. As well as myself of course.

I will never go so far as to actually throw a stone or a broken object at the window of the old woman's boudoir. Instead I will beat my own forehead whenever everything becomes a little too unbearable. As I have always done. Then I feel I am my father, who used to beat his forehead quite often. Quite seriously too. He used to start all of a sudden. One could never tell what would provoke him into that outburst. My mother couldn't do anything but watch, transfixed. I used to feel as if I was watching a beast in agony. Perhaps it is in homage to those indelible scenes that I still pretend to fly into an outrage. In reality I do not feel outraged by anything now. I cannot. Besides, my forehead-beating would not make me miserable now. Not even physically. Besides, there is not much strength left in my hands. Nor many veins in my forehead. My beating amounts to no more than a faint stroking. Which reminds me of the women mourners of my decrepit childhood ages ago. They attended every funeral and participated in the ritual breast-thigh-beating, but all they really did was caress their breasts and thighs. Their gestures seemed suggestive. They always aroused me. No, my forehead-beating doesn't give me enough pain now. It is not worth the effort any more. Except that it does bring back memories of the times when I really enjoyed my fury and the pain it caused me. My forehead was often corrugated by dark blue veins after every bout. And for days after that I used to be ravished by shooting pains in my hands and head. I inherited this habit from my parents. My mother often competed with my father. They stood face to face and beat their foreheads with all their fury, their eyes wide open, their lips sealed. My father always won.

I had to cut the above recollection short, because of the arrows of anger shooting out of my toenails. My arrows of anger! The last breaths of a burnt-out beast!

I think I have finally reached a point beyond guilt and repentance. But if I have, what am I whining about? I am not whining about anything. Except that it is futile to wait for a phase which . . . no, I won't complete this sentence.

I feel as hollow as I used to a hundred years ago. I think exactly as I did a hundred years ago. My bones have dried up, my skin has withered, my teeth have fallen out, my skull has collapsed, my energy has evaporated, but underneath all these deteriorations I can still experience the same empty anxiety, the same absence of direction, the same presence of pain that I have been experiencing ever since my birth.

This piece of rotten insight should be punished by slow death.

To go on with my story. After I had slipped my shirt on, I repeated—So you are kicking me out, are you?

Obviously, it was an unnecessary question. Actually, it wasn't a question. It was a desperate and, as it turned out, ineffective way of probing her, of imploring her to change her mind. She nodded her head once and stood, implacably, waiting for me to leave. She is full of flaws—for instance her habit of walking with her legs wide apart, or her unbelievable ignorance about the world outside her own small town—but I like the way she relies on gestures instead of words on special occasions.

I asked—That's why you invited me over?

She nodded her head again.

I asked—You mean it is all over between us unless I agree to your proposal?

She nodded her head again.

I asked—Are you sure?

She nodded her head again.

I asked—Are you serious?

She nodded her head again.

I asked—You mean you are never going to come over to my house?

She nodded her head again.

I knew what she meant by her last nod but I had begun to enjoy my cross-examination. So I asked—You mean you will?

She shook her head.

I asked—You mean, you can do without me?

She nodded her head again.

I asked—You mean it is all that easy for you?

She nodded her head again.

I asked—You mean either marriage or nothing?

She nodded her head again.

I asked—Are you an old woman or an idiotic teenager?

She stayed still.

I asked—Why didn't you propose earlier?

She stayed still.

I asked—Were you afraid I'd refuse?

She nodded her head again.

I asked—Did you hope that I'd propose?

She nodded her head again.

I am sick of this cross-examination, which went on, I seem to remember, for several hours. I saw both of us with an impartial eye and realized that her proposal and my refusal were equally ridiculous. Before leaving her house I wanted to cast a final glance at everything in the room. Her household effects are far more elegant than mine. But who needs elegance at my age in my condition!

I said—Do you know you are an old-fashioned reactionary?

She nodded her head again.

I asked—You mean even at your age you think it sinful to sleep with a man of my age?

She nodded her head again.

I asked—Aren't you ashamed of yourself?

She shook her head.

I asked—So you are kicking me out, are you?

She nodded her head again.

Her bed was between the two of us. I started advancing toward her inch by inch around the bed. At that time my movements were not quite as slow as they are now. If my movements now can be called movements; if my movements then could be called movements. Whether they could be or not, they were movements of sorts, painful and unsure. Nevertheless, I was advancing with the measured grimness of an assassin or a rapist toward a weak and vulnerable victim. I am sure the same analogy must have struck the old woman's wrinkled mind, for she stared at me even as she retreated one step at a time. The pace of her retreat was a little faster than the pace of my advance, because I could see the distance between us increasing inch by inch. I had a great urge to leap across the distance and, putting my claws around her neck, ask her—Will you take that proposal back, or won't you? But there is a great gap between the urge to leap and the actual leap. A gap I couldn't have bridged. Otherwise I am sure I'd have shaken her up. Fear might have restored her to sense. And she might have been in my bed now, or I in hers, both of us laughing and panting. It is odd that even now the idea of intercourse with her doesn't make me nauseous. On the contrary, both my mind and body would be quite happy to have her make my bed malodorous with her ardour. If this is not love or lunacy, what is it? Many a time my right hand rises to reach for the phone, but I manage to restrain it with my left. I am afraid she must have clean forgotten me while waiting for her end. Or perhaps she has fallen in love with another old man. A little better than me perhaps. Some native of this little town. Someone who speaks her language. Perhaps she is enjoying herself with him right now. Perhaps she is telling him all about me. Perhaps he is asking her—Was that bastard by any chance harder than I am; is that why you keep talking about him? Perhaps she is teasing him by her silence.

I was suddenly seized by laughter a while back. The slightest error on my part would have turned that laughter into a tearing cough.

Dying Alone

So I decided to stop and wait for it to end. And, now, I am in no mood to carry on. But I will carry on.

No, there is none other. Either in her life or in mine. I don't know about her but this thought gives me a sense of fearful freedom. *There is none other*! I remember the tune. I've lost the rest of the words. I think I'll interrupt myself and hum this tune for the rest of the day. *There is none other*! I'll hum it like that old songstress I suddenly remember who died humming some tune similar to this. I don't remember her name but if I try I may be able to recall her tattered face. And the profound emptiness of her voice. But why should I try? Whenever I try to recall someone from my past over there, all I am able to evoke is a shadowy figure trembling past my eyes. *There is none other*! I should perhaps dial the old woman's number; then, as soon as she hollers hello, I should burst into my song: *There is none other*! And then hang up. I have not risen above naughty impulses. Even at my age. *There is none other*! Ages ago, when I first arrived here, when I hadn't yet taken possession of this house or vice versa, when I hadn't yet accepted my alienhood, when I was still raw relatively, I used to latch on to an old curse or a couplet and repeat it for days in order to assuage my nostalgia. Now I don't do that. I don't have to. This snatch of a song has taken me back to those days. To that other place.

There is none other! I have chanted this mantra all day today. Now the night is drawing nigh. If I don't stop I may have to chant it all night tonight. Perhaps the rest of the words will come back to me during the stillness of the night. I notice I continue to distinguish my days from the nights. Perhaps I'll discover the complete text in some old book or notebook. But do I really need the complete text? *There is none other*! This sounds complete enough. The essence of my angst. Someday, I mean certainly before the end, I will destroy all my books and notebooks. It will take some time. It will also take some trouble. There'll be the danger of breaking my wrists or ribs if I strain too much. Perhaps I should burn them. In a bonfire. Along with my letters. Along with my clothes. I could throw myself also into the same bonfire. My house, my household effects, and I myself. All consumed by the same bonfire! An attractive idea! People will attribute the fire to a burning butt or a bad wire. Perhaps the old woman's house will also be burned along with mine. I have often closed my eyes and seen myself lying on a pyre, waiting for someone to come and light it. It has been ages since I last saw a house or a householder burning. I can't even remember how a burning matchstick smells. Had there been one beside me just now, I would have struck it and satisfied at least this simple desire. I have an ancient and intimate relationship with fire and smoke. A little more ancient and intimate with smoke than with fire. There was a time when the very memory of smoke used to tickle my nose and stiffen my eyes. Almost everyone has an ancient and intimate relationship with fire and smoke. Also with water and dust. Also with air. But at this time it is fire I am yearning for. Pure fire. Red-yellow-white. When the old woman still brought her odour to my house, we often shared a cigar after a bout of mutual beastliness. I couldn't help howling with laughter whenever I saw the fat cigar stuck in her mouth. Before putting it in my own mouth, I never forgot to wipe it on the sly, for she was very sensitive.

So here she is again. She won't leave me alone until I tell her story to the end.

I asked—Shall I leave then?

She nodded her head again.

I think I asked her the same question a couple more times because I hoped my repetition would wear her out and she'd change her mind. But I am sick of that scene. No more about those few final moments. Suffice it to say that I left her house. I don't remember what I did first on reaching my own. I don't remember what I thought. Even if I did, I wouldn't record my thoughts here. To tell the truth, I remember everything. And I wouldn't mind recording everything here. On entering my house, the first thing I did was to sit on the toilet and talk to myself. For a long time. I don't remember what I told myself. To tell the truth, I remember everything. Had I not, my face wouldn't be suffused with shame at this moment. Suffused with shame! It has been ages since I last used this phrase. I wish a few more ages had passed before I did so.

I am getting irritated. What less does anyone expect from a mole of my age? Perhaps I've lost my cool because of the memory of my final moments with the old woman. When did I ever have any cool? Where? Now, perhaps, I should get up and go to the bathroom. In times gone by, sometimes, I saw her from my bathroom window lying stark naked on her bed, absorbed in an unmentionable pastime. Frequently I flatter myself with the vain thought that she often stands behind a closed window, her eye clamped to a carefully carved hole, watching me as I stand or sit and suffer in my bathroom. My ego is still alive. I am quite angry at this moment. Which is why this fit of awful coughing.

Whenever my happiness or unhappiness exceeds a certain limit, this awful cough attacks my lungs and ribs. Unlike other old people, I have no phlegm in my system, so I can't just spit something out and feel a little relief. I see a few drops of my spittle on the page, looking like dirty dewdrops. My eyes are full of foul water. One of my hands is trembling; the other will as soon as I let it—for the time being it is holding my head as well as it can. Had there been a hidden observer around, he would have thought: Poor old wretch! To tell the truth, appearances apart, I am happy to have this cough. But for it, my limbs wouldn't be as active as they are. I have noticed that laughing and coughing prolongs one's life. I am suddenly beset by a scene from my boyhood. I see a dried-up old woman sitting, her head between her knees, outside a mud hut, coughing; around her is a circle of half-naked dirty children, stamping their feet to the beat of her coughing, and shouting—More, more! People often told one another in that town that after each fit of coughing God increased that old woman's age by one more year. As a kind of reward, perhaps, or an act of divine malice. I don't know why I thought of that old woman. To tell the truth, I do.

Two

He always comes in the evening whenever he does. Exactly when the day is breathing its last and my heart is about to break. He never forewarns me. Which is why almost every evening a dim apprehension of his arrival never leaves my mind and body. The moment he arrives, he asks in a loud voice—So you are still alive, are you? Its loudness apart, his inquiry is free of any note of surprise or joy or anger. As if he has risen above ordinary human notes. During the course of my long and blasted life all sorts of oddballs have inflicted their moans and miseries on my unwilling ears and have, in turn, lent their unwilling ears to my moans and miseries, but it has been ages since I withdrew from the world at large and took refuge in this capacious curse of a house in this remote town in this alien state. It has been ages since all my contacts with others dried up. Most of my old friends have died; the rest must have been devoured by space and time. I like to think of them as depraved victims of malevolent cosmic forces. I am not sure whether I ever had any wife or children, or, if I did, how many I did. I do not know where they are, if they are. It is quite probable I derived some pleasure or pain by thinking of them once upon a time—if they were, even if they weren't—but now I seldom have the desire to think of them. Whenever I do all I experience is a strange stillness. Of the kind I never experience when I think of anything or anyone else. Perhaps I can dig out, if I try, some old notebook containing a clear record of their existence or non-existence, of whether I ever remembered them in the past. Perhaps some evening they too, or those of them who have survived my long neglect of them, will suddenly descend upon me and say—So you are still alive! Sometimes in some insane moment I can't help imagining that this old woman is a wife of mine, now in disguise, and that wretch who always comes in the evening whenever he does is a son of mine, now in disguise. But it is an insane thought, I know. I don't have the nerve to smile at it.

When both of us were middle-aged, he resorted to all kinds of antics to prove that he was superior to me. I don't remember those antics in detail. I wouldn't have gone into them even if I did. To tell the truth, I remember everything. I pretend to be forgetful only in order to spare myself the nuisance of recording my memories. I never forget anything. As I have asserted before. He used to taunt me with this—like a dark angel perched on my shoulder: So you are still alive? At that time his question didn't sound exactly like a question, but rather a statement of a miserable fact. I was able to ignore it. Soon enough we would plunge into a violent exchange of views about other issues, broad as well as narrow, mostly broad, fundamental as well as superficial, mostly fundamental. He used to call himself the Emperor of Fundamental Issues: Peace and Void, Pain and Others, Family and Alienation, Incurable Boredom, Death and After-death, Matter and Mind, Consciousness and Silence, Noise and Music, Darkness and Light, Heaven and Hades. In those exchanges we were always on opposite sides. On any given issue it was difficult to predict which side he would be on. Sometimes, in an effort to unhinge him, I would switch in the middle of an argument to his side, but he was always able to switch to mine without batting an eye. Apart from those fundamental issues, he also sometimes surprised me with a shower of personal questions—How long does it take you to come these days? Can you describe the odour of the woman you are sleeping with now? When will you rise above all this nonsense?

What will become of you? Why don't you commit suicide? When will you admit that you are ordinary?

I have chanted many hymns to him. I will chant some more. I can't claim I have understood him. Perhaps I never will. Thanks more to his ineffableness than to my failings.

He visited me again yesterday. At that time I was sitting on the floor of this very room, rubbing one of my longest rosaries. My head was swinging in between my knees and my knees were pushing into my cheeks. I often adopt this uncomfortable posture. Because changing it is so painful, I am able to kill the desire to change it. Of course, this posture itself is no less painful. But when I was still over there, I saw innumerable old people, particularly beggars, sitting peacefully in this painful posture, announcing their pains. So I favour it now, here. The postures I saw over there are not only engraved on my mind but also insist on getting translated into my bodily gestures.

As soon as he came in yesterday, he enquired as usual—So you are still alive, are you?

His voice, as usual, didn't express any surprise or joy or pain. I felt as usual that he was trying to raise the ghost of one of his fundamental issues. My body began to burn. I wish I weren't being merely metaphorical. I started rubbing my rosary more nervously. My rosaries are not merely metaphorical. I am sick of them. Were I an adept old-fashioned storyteller, capable of describing everything with the requisite patience, I would have described each bead of my rosary, each touch of my weary fingers. But any such description is beyond me. Thank God!

As soon as he spoke, several shades arose around me, and I felt I had been arrested.

This doesn't ring true. It isn't even if it does. I hear a note of moaning in my voice. I don't want to waste the rest of my life in moans. I want to breathe my last, not moaning or screaming, but laughing, absurdly, so that, if anyone should care to recall my last

Dying Alone

face after I'm gone, he should see a toothless old child, his eyes closed, his mouth open—emitting light. Obviously I am recalling some picture seen centuries ago. Anyway. I have another great desire—I want to be rid of this awful word: anyway.

—So you are still alive.

I didn't raise my head. Nor did I stop rubbing my rosary. His voice was lustrous, as always, but even without raising my head I could guess that his body had become a little more battered. I couldn't possibly have raised my head. He was standing at an angle, and if I had tried to raise my head in a hurry, I would have strained, perhaps broken, my neck. His arrival did not disturb my reverie. These days, whenever I am thinking of my old woman or my old body or any of my favorite rosaries, I feel as lively as a rake. I should feel ashamed of it, but I don't. To tell the truth, there are times when I almost forget, while rubbing some of my rosaries, that I am a doddering old fool, an outcast, an exile, a solitary—outwardly scarred and inwardly bruised; friendless—who has wasted the better part of his blasted life in this alien arctic wasteland, who has recently stopped pining for his native sun-dried desert over there because he wants to spend his last few years in beatitude rather than in useless yearning. Of course, I never forget anything. I cannot. But there are occasions when I have to use the expression, *I almost forget etc.*

—So you are still alive.

I kept quiet and continued to rub my rosary.

—Stop rubbing your rosary.

I stopped rubbing my rosary but I didn't answer his question.

—Has there been any change in your fear of death?

I shook my head.

—Won't you speak?

I shook my head.

—Do you spend all your time sitting like this?

I shook my head.

—What else do you do?

I kept quiet.

—Have you stopped speaking?
I shook my head.
—Are you happy?
I shook my head.
—Are you unhappy?
I shook my head.
—Are you still as scared of me as before?
I shook my head.
—Are you still scared of me?
I shook my head.
—Are you scared of me?
I shook my head.
—You aren't scared of me?
I shook my head.
—Do you say no to every question?
I shook my head.
—Do you want to die?
I shook my head.
—Do you want to live?
I shook my head.
—Do you want to become incognito like me?
I shook my head.
—Do you regard me as your friend?
I shook my head.
—Do you remember the times when I used to exclaim: What will become of me!
I shook my head.
—Aren't you being untruthful?
I shook my head.
—Are you being truthful?
I shook my head.
—Don't you get bored with yourself?
I shook my head.
—Are you still involved with the old woman?
I shook my head.
—Don't you ever get tired of yourself?
I shook my head.

—Have you become sufficient unto yourself?
I shook my head.
—Will you die in this house?
I kept quiet but hoped he would guess I didn't know where I would die.
—Do you want to commit suicide?
I kept quiet but hoped he would guess I wanted to but wouldn't.
—Would you like to return to whatever it was over there?
I kept quiet and hoped he would guess I was saying yes and no.
—Why do you rub your rosary?
I kept quiet but hoped he would guess I was saying: To pass the time.
—What sort of nightmares do you have these days?
I kept quiet and hoped he would guess I didn't want to tell him.
—Have you ever looked in a mirror recently?
I shook my head.
—Is that why you are so arrogant?
I shook my head.
—Do you want me to leave?
I kept quiet and hoped he would guess I was saying: I don't care.
—Don't you want to ask me anything?
I shook my head.
—Do you know everything?
I shook my head.
—Do you know what is happening in the world outside yourself?
I kept quiet and hoped he would guess I was saying: My knowing or not knowing would not make any difference to the world outside myself.
—You are determined to remain aloof?
I kept quiet and hoped he would guess I was saying that, at the limit I had reached, both my aloofness and involvement were equally pointless, but I wasn't determined because I couldn't be,

although I wished I did because then I wouldn't have had him badgering me at that moment.

—Do you want another chance?

I shook my head.

—Another life?

I shook my head.

—Do you miss me?

I kept quiet and thought: Is he just being presumptuous? Or is he really afraid I have cut myself loose from him? But he can't be so stupid! I wish he was! Then I wouldn't have been so badly bruised by his questions. Then I wouldn't have missed him. Then I wouldn't have looked forward secretly to his visits.

—Have you started stinking to yourself?

I kept quiet and hoped he would guess that I was thinking: I have become immune to your malice now, or at least that is what I would like you to think, even though I know you have always managed to think the opposite of what I want you to.

—I meant to ask if your body has started to stink?

I kept quiet because I knew he knew I had understood what he meant.

—Do you know this is our last meeting?

I gave a start but kept quiet and hoped he would guess I knew that that wasn't our last meeting, because I didn't want that to be our last meeting, because I wanted that our last meeting should be closer to our end.

—Do you know that I have come to prepare you for the end?

I kept quiet and hoped he would guess that I didn't depend on him to prepare me for the end, or, at least, I would never admit I did.

His tone throughout this colloquy was like that of a bureaucrat talking to an inferior with a blend of bantering and sneering. From my posture, not to speak of my silence and my swinging head, any observer would have inferred he was the master, I the slave. Even at this age our relationship rests on the same unevenness it used to when we were young. I felt very sour as I thought of this. I had a great desire to be his equal, to face him without fear. I had never done that even over there. Of course I often had the desire then, but was always able to extinguish it. Even over there he came, whenever he did, at dawn or dusk, and I always had a lurking doubt whether he was he or someone else. Even when he came and settled down in my house for varying periods, we rarely sat or stood face to face, presumably because we didn't want to end our mutual reserve. Occasionally we slept in the same bed. Facing away from each other throughout the night.

But why am I recording all this here? For whom? I need to raise these questions every now and then. In order to be able to rake my memories. In order to be able to suppress them. Otherwise I would be forever lost in the jungle of my past.

I started turning toward him even as I sat, but my movement was so slow that I wasn't sure whether I was actually turning or only getting ready to do so. If I had only been turning my head, if I could have turned my head only, I might have succeeded in facing him sooner or later despite my slow pace. But I was turning my entire body, from top to bottom, because it has become so stiff that every limb is dependent upon every other for the slightest movement. Which is why I am unable to act on any impulse now, because, by the time I coax all of my body into acquiescence, my impulse is over. Which is why I spend most of my time in coaxing my body into acquiescence now. It takes me so long to start any movement that, by the time I am ready, I have forgotten what that movement was going to be. Which is why most of the time I just lie here or there like a withered stump.

I started turning all the same to him as I sat. Like a half-alive leper to a miracle worker. I was afraid he would lose his patience any moment and shout: I am off. Even though I was afraid of it, I would have welcomed his announcing his abrupt departure. If I had gotten up before starting to turn, turning might have become considerably, or at least slightly, easier. But getting up is a nearly impossible task in itself. When I am sitting, most of my limbs are fast asleep. Before getting up, or, in fact, starting to make any movement, I have to awaken them. Which is quite a tedium. By the time I succeed—or imagine I have succeeded—in awakening one up, another I had awakened after considerable effort has already gone back to sleep. I haven't yet discovered the skill or acquired the strength to awaken all my sleeping limbs at the same time. What actually happens most of the time is that, in my efforts to awaken my sleeping limbs, I invariably forget why I started trying to do so.

Besides, I call my sitting sitting only for the sake of convenience. Just as I do my standing standing. Just as I do my lying lying. Just as I do my walking walking. Just as I do my turning turning. Even so, I was turning as best I could in order to be able to face up to him without fear.

The question may be raised: Why do I sit at all, particularly in this posture, the changing of which is so arduous and painful? This question deserves many answers. All unsatisfactory. I'll offer one right now. Before coming to rust in this little town in this alien state, I saw, over there, on every path, numerous old people, all beggarly like myself, appealing to the nobler instincts of an endless stream of callous passers-by. I don't know for sure whether in reality it was exactly like this; but my memory is certainly populated by hordes of helpless old people; it resounds with their rending pleas. There were quite a few lepers among them. Their noses still nibble at my sleep every night. About half of them were women. Many of them were hunchbacks. Many of them were blind. A number of them were cripples. I often watched them from a safe enough distance. Whenever it became unavoidable to approach or pass by them, I felt as if someone was rubbing my nose in the gutter. I imagine this posture, in which I often sit and rub my rosaries, is in memory of the misery I witnessed over there. My old age has a lot to do with it too. It doesn't take much effort now to collapse on my haunches. Some of my joints are suitable only for bending. And, because I am nearly weightless now, sitting on my haunches is far less painful than almost any other posture. Which, of course, doesn't mean it is not painful enough.

Dying Alone

So then there I was, turning slowly to him as I sat and rubbed my rosary.

As I rub my rosaries I don't murmur a mantra. I rub my rosaries because it helps empty my mind. Some people rock, some hum, some shake their heads to music, some groan, some pace. Most ordinary people have to do something in order to shake their bodies off their minds, in order to rise above their ruins, in order to forget. I rub my rosaries. Turn and turn about. Since I was rubbing one as I turned toward him, the pace of my turning was even slower than it would have been otherwise.

Sometimes I mimic the pleas of those beggars I observed over there. Just as some people hum old tunes in order to haunt old times. Sometimes my mimicry rises to music, I forget I am in this monster of a house, dying from day to day; the walls become invisible, and I feel as if I am already in a state where every moan is melodious. This feeling doesn't last long, but as long as it does I feel I have lost my body and boredom. Later on when I try to reduce it all to words I feel as if I am trying to drape the air.

When turning and rubbing the rosary at the same time became impossible, I put the rosary aside. I placed my palms on the floor, put all my barely existing weight on them, and started to turn ever so slightly. I was actually trying to execute an adroit movement an old legless beggar used to carry out over there. That bastard, towering over me, was perhaps smiling at my efforts and thinking of the same smart beggar.

And then suddenly he started to speak in a grey voice, which reached me like a ghostly murmur coming from a great distance. My entire attention was absorbed by my aching trunk and bottom. My face was firm with pain. If he hadn't started listening to himself, he might have helped me. In fact he could have easily shifted his position and squatted down in front of me. Then I wouldn't have had even to lift my head. The least he could have done was to remain silent. But I know that helping me, or squatting down in front of me, or remaining silent, would have caused him the same degree of pain and same amount of effort that I was experiencing in trying to turn toward him. He might even have broken into two if he had tried to sit down. My desire to see him breaking into two is old and ineradicable but I doubt if it will ever be satisfied.

His major flaw is his tendency to preach. Even when he is silent he is not. It is largely thanks to this flaw that he has survived so far: I am sure he'll also die when he does because of this. But he will not die before I do. His effort is to outlive me, mine to outlive him. Which explains why both of us are still alive. Which leads me to believe that we will perhaps die on the same day at the same moment.

So I kept turning and he kept talking. I can always anticipate which sermon he will deliver on what occasion. Of late, however, he has been delivering the same sermon on every occasion. I can, therefore, ignore him even without listening to him. Sometimes I feel he always tells me what I want to hear. This alarms me. I don't want our mutual differences to fade into the illusion that there are no mutual differences between the two of us. By now our ages have reached that enormity and our faces that anonymity that no observer, howsoever keen, will be able to tell at a glance who is who, or who is speaking and who thinking, or who is the owner of the house and who the visitor. Had there been a hidden observer, he might have thought he was singing while I was dancing, weirdly, to his tune. This thought stopped me in my turning. I felt like reaching out, seizing him by his ankles, and bringing him down to the floor with a wild pull. I was deterred by the thought that he might fall without, however, dying, in which case I would have to put up with him for the rest of his life, or mine, or ours.

He was saying in his toothless voice—You don't know. You don't know anything. How would you! All you worry about even at your age is your body. Otherwise, you wouldn't be in this condition. You have always shut your eyes to reality. Tell me if you haven't! But you can't tell me anything. I know. You don't. You are so close to the end, but your unawareness, your ignorance, knows no end. Otherwise you wouldn't be here. But you won't admit. I know you won't. You don't know anything. Have you seen your face in the mirror lately? Tell me! Even if you did, I'm sure you saw nothing. Even if you saw, you wouldn't admit. Even if you admitted, you wouldn't fully. I know. I know you. You don't know. You don't know me. Your longing hasn't ended. Even now. Even at your age. It hasn't become less. Even now. Even at your age. After I leave, you will start mocking me and my speech. I know. I don't know why I suffer for you. Do I suffer for you or not? Tell me! But you won't. Don't pretend to be deaf. Please! I know you can hear me very well. You are, of course, ignoring what you hear. Only utterly useless laughter pleases you. Even now. Even at your age. After all this intimacy you still regard me as your enemy. Do you or not? Tell me! But now, perhaps, you regard me as nothing. There was a time when you used to fear me. Perhaps that fear too was false. Otherwise you would have acted on at least one of my instructions. There was a time when you used to feel ashamed of yourself whenever you saw me. Perhaps that shame too was false. Otherwise you wouldn't be wasting away this final phase of your life in this house rubbing your rosaries. You would have been preparing yourself to face death. You'll perhaps retort: What else am I doing now? No you won't retort. You'll continue to insult me by your silence. You want to assert yourself and be my equal. But have you forgotten that I am bigger than you, better than you, taller than you, that you owe all your airs to me? I'll never let you forget; I'll never let you forget anything. Do you really think that this house is your citadel? That you'll go straight from here to heaven? You're wrong. You don't know anything. I feel sorry for you. But if you don't desist from your senile lechery, my sorrow will change into anger. And you know me when I am angry. Do you or not? I am urging you to desist. Again and again. All my life I've saved you from superficial pleasures so that you may be able to devote all your energy to fundamental issues. Which, of course, couldn't have been resolved either by you or me. Which, in fact, can never be resolved. But to resolve which, to continue to try to resolve which, is the destiny of people like you and me. All your life you have been trying to lose me. And now I am as old and useless as you, but even now....

When I heard him collapsing into this tired tone, I was so relieved that I resumed my turning with a grimmer determination. His voice again became remote and phantasmal. Let him drivel on, I thought, what do I care, sooner or later he is bound to talk himself into a mawkish mole, and then he'll stop, on his own, or start apologizing to me. I was determined not to utter a word until I had turned all the way to him and looked him in the eye.

I am used to all his threats. He is used to all my silences. We have known each other almost ever since we were born. We have been attached to each other ever since. Despite many long phases of mutual alienation. He has had a finger in all my follies. I have had a wing in all his flights. All his reproaches are directed, in part, at his own inadequacy. All my inadequacies, in part, are derived from his. We are convinced, each in his own heart, that we'll remain forever mutually indispensable and inseparable. To tell the truth, for the last so many years, our mutual differences have been fading so fast that our bickering now is no more than a hangover of our previous, more fundamental, disputes and our habit of resolving them by howling at each other. Which is why his reproofs have lost their old edge. He cannot add to or decrease my pains by any speech; he cannot make me walk out of this house in search of panaceas. He knows both of us have reached the limit, that the only liberation either of us can look forward to is through death. If, despite this, he doesn't stop needling me, it is because of his lifelong habit of prodding every inert beast. My experience has been that, if I keep quiet long enough, he talks himself into a tantrum, begins to contradict himself at every sentence, and finally becomes quite pathetic. Like a clumsy child entangled in the cord of his kite dragging its beak along the ground as he tries to run out of the entanglement. I feel happy when I see his pride having a fall. I shouldn't but I do. I shouldn't because, after all, if, at my age, I can't feel sorry for him, and myself, and for the millions of other old people like him and me, I shouldn't at least gloat over his, or my own, or their, fall. In other words I am not indifferent enough. I shouldn't grieve over the inadequacy of my indifference. I

Dying Alone

shouldn't grieve over anything. These injunctions also have their source in him. When he is not around, or I imagine he is not, I don't debilitate myself with self-exhortation. I only pass or endure the time.

Does it mean I am still subservient to him? That we haven't become one yet? Or even almost one? Can he even now lure me into the bogs I thought I had left far behind?

I kept turning to him like a tired sunflower. Trying to ignore his words and my weariness. Hoping he wouldn't disappear before I completed my turn; fearing he would. As he had so many times before.

Then I heard him attacking me from another angle. I was startled. I stopped turning in order to listen to his harangue.

—I will not accept that your revulsion has risen to the level of non-attachment. That you have risen too high now to discriminate between this and that. Between here and there. That, while dragging your bottom along the floor, you are never ravaged by memories of your misery over there. That you have exorcised your past. I will not accept that you have become an adept. That your alienation has ended. That your torment has nothing to do with your banishment from there. That you are unafraid of an anonymous death in this house. That you have ceased to yearn for immortality. I will not accept that you have grown altogether independent of me. That you do not see me in your nightmares. That you have begun to love your loneliness. That you are in love with the old woman next door. I will not accept that you are so happy in this house that you are never wrenched by the hope of renouncing it one day and standing on the edge of a deserted road and moaning ceaselessly. I will not accept that you alienated yourself from other inane attachments only in order to hole up here and end your life like a crippled animal, rubbing your rosaries, blackening your notebooks, nursing your nauseas. I will not accept, I will not.

I could see he was running out of rage. I could also see that he didn't intimidate me any more. I would have been overwhelmed by the perception that he was still persisting in his efforts to liberate me from my lingering attachment to matter, had I not been convinced that I would be nowhere if I let him turn me out of my last lair. At the same time I wasn't altogether unaffected by the alternative he offered—the edge of a deserted road. So I resumed my slow turn. I will ask him after seeing him face to face: So now you want me to leave this house and go stand on the edge of a deserted road? Like a homeless hunchback? Can you draw me a picture of that road? He will imagine I have stopped resisting him. He will start smiling. Then I'll change my tone and start shouting my defiance at him. He'll choke on his smile, like someone whose teeth have fallen into his throat.

I couldn't help laughing at my vision of his discomfiture. My laughter couldn't help declining into a hacking cough. Now I was squirming like a frog out of water. I don't remember how long this lasted. But, when I recovered a bit, I shut my mouth and fists tight, clenched my gums, and felt my temples throbbing. Most of my other limbs have lost their liveliness but my temples continue to throb on special occasions. Presently I was only panting instead of laughing or coughing. My eyes were closed. Some stuff was oozing out of them. I wish I could call it blood. I have always wanted to shed tears of blood. I have always imagined that heroes shed tears of blood. I am indulging in an old pleasantry. At my own expense of course. It gives me a peculiar personal pain. I touched that moisture coming out of my eyes and decided it was neither blood nor water but some other liquid, a little sticky, that perhaps oozed out of the eyes of monsters of my age on special occasions. I closed my eyes.

When I opened them I found I had turned all the way round, thanks perhaps to my cough, but he wasn't there. I shouldn't have been surprised because he has played this mean trick before. Many a time. Reducing me to doubt that he had ever come. That he had uttered the words I had heard. I thought he had perhaps changed his place and was standing behind me once again, waiting for me to start turning once again. I couldn't have even if I had wanted to.

Besides, I wasn't sure he wouldn't change his place again the moment I completed my turn, assuming that he was still around and had not altogether disappeared, assuming also that he had been there, that he hadn't been a figment of my fear. I could have shouted: Where are you, you devil, show your face to me, even if you have no face to show! Or: If you didn't want to appear to me, why did you come? Or: If you didn't come, how is it that I heard you? Or: I am ready to renounce this house and go stand on the edge of your deserted road! Or: Aren't you ashamed of playing hide-and-seek with me at my age, at your age? Or: I am dying and you are still not through with your practical jokes! Or: If you don't want to see me face to face, the least you can do is to say something! I could have attempted many other taunts. But I wasn't sure that I would have been able to produce anything more than a mean mumble. Besides, above all, I wasn't sure that he was still there, that he had ever been there, that he wasn't a darling of my own delusions. I don't know for how long I stared at his absence before starting to debate whether I should try to get up or not. I don't know for how long I debated that before deciding not to. I don't know whether I decided not to or just didn't. I don't know after how long my temples stopped throbbing, my clenched gums came unclenched, the faint depressions caused by my nails in my palms disappeared, and I began to feel either drowsy or dizzy. But, perhaps, before doing that, I had the urge to urinate, which I did, sitting, but I don't know how long it took me to do it. After I had peered into the tiny yellow lake between my feet, I dragged myself away from it. I don't know for how long I savoured my smell before I drowsed off. After a minute, or perhaps a second, when I opened my eyes, I felt as if a whole century had gone by. Though my age may not have liberated me from anything else, it has from sleep. I am happy. I want to die fully awake. So that I can misguide the coming generations by my memoirs, so that it can be said of me after I'm gone that I slogged at my saga until the end. I am a sly old man. I believe all old people are sly more or less. Take, for example, him to whom I devoted so much time and turning and whom I couldn't even see.

Three

It was a couple of days, or perhaps years, or perhaps minutes, or perhaps months, or perhaps weeks, or perhaps seconds—although it could have been twenty or twenty-five or four or three or thirteen days, or years, or minutes, or months, or weeks, or seconds—back that I was sitting in a room upstairs. The one whose one window opens on the street. I was picking my nose when I saw a sleek black limousine, looking like a sleek black cat, parked in front of the old woman's house. Ordinarily this street is so deserted in the morning and in the evening and at noon and at night that, at first, I didn't believe my eyes. I closed and rubbed them viciously. Then, as I tried to open them, I learnt they wished to be rubbed a little more. Had I not needed them, I wouldn't have complied with their wish. When I opened them, after rubbing them even more viciously, I saw two sleek black limousines shimmering before me. Then they gradually became one. I couldn't but believe my eyes now.

My eyes contain no water now but their vision has become even keener. Perhaps at the expense of the rest of my faculties.

Dying Alone

The few houses still standing along this street are occupied by people of my, and the old woman's, extreme age. From outside, perhaps, these houses seem deserted. Especially during the day. During the night most of them are lit. But in each of them lives a solitary old person. Awaiting, or, if you will, resisting death. Or so at least I'd like to imagine. Some of these old people are subjecting their lives to a final and furious analysis. Or so at least I'd like to again imagine. They have been abandoned by their dear ones. Or so at least I'd like to imagine yet again. No one ever visits them. Nor does any one of them ever stir out. On business or pleasure. Or at least I haven't seen anyone coming in or going out. Or if I have I don't remember. The one who suddenly descends on me every now and then doesn't count. Because I have serious doubts about his arrivals and departures. I concede that my conjectures can be wrong. Because only one window of only one room in my house opens on the street. And all I can see through it is a narrow strip of the road. For even this window doesn't actually open on the street. I mean I can't open it. All I can do is press my thick nose against its thick pane and see that which I can. Besides, I do not spend all my time at this window. My house has two storeys and several rooms. I am seldom in any room or corner of my house of my own will, which is ruled by the caprices and constraints of my body. It is, therefore, quite likely that when I am in some other room or corner of my house, at some other window, or even when I am in this room but am busy with some other inactivity, this street begins to run like a sore. In fact I am willing to concede that all my conjectures about this street, about the houses along this street, about their occupants, are wrong. It is quite likely that, apart from my house and that of the old woman's, every house along this street is bursting with life. Of body and mind.

Anyway. Before that day, I never saw any sleek black limousine parked in front of the old woman's house. It is quite likely that I did and have forgotten—for the time being. There is no limit to likelihood. If this likelihood hadn't made all my conjectures suspect, I might have ventured a few more. For instance, that the old people living in these houses have made the same arrangements for their daily needs that I have. It is quite likely that I made this conjecture and then killed it. Somebody brings me whatever I need. Once a month. Or perhaps once a year. Or perhaps once a week. He puts the bundle behind the front door, and pays himself from the cash always lying about the door. I have never seen the fellow. Nor have I ever desired to. I don't know whether he has ever seen me. Nor have I ever wanted to. It is quite likely that a long time ago I entered into a complicated contract with an honest general merchant for a regular supply of bare essentials. In exchange, of course, for an extra consideration. I might have stipulated that his delivery man was not to see me. Or be seen by me. That, even if he did, he was to pretend he hadn't. That he was to come, open the door already open, deliver the things to the hall, pick up the money, and leave immediately. Not once have I run out of any of the bare essentials. But it is also quite likely that I did many times but never noticed. Or that I noticed every time but never remembered. It is quite likely that, whenever I ran out of any of the bare essentials, I also ran out of my need for them. There is no limit to likelihood. It is quite likely that all the other old people on this street are young, that they are frequent visitors to one another's houses, that they are fond of playing bridge or gin rummy, that they are fond of long conversations on the phone, that they are fond of fucking one another. It is quite likely that after it was all over between the two of us, the old woman latched on to some other younger old man. But even he must have left her now. Otherwise that sleek black limousine wouldn't be parked in front of her house. It is quite likely that that limousine is not a limousine, that that limousine is not. . . . No it is not. There is a limit to likelihood.

During the seven months that this street is buried under snow, I am sure no old person stirs out. Or only those who are already dead do. The thought of stirring out has often crossed my mind, too, but never stayed there. Watching the snow from behind the door or window is enough to kill me slowly. The pleasures of a slow killing are intense enough for me. I don't want to plunge to my death in snow. I am not suggesting that no one ever passes along this street when it is under snow. Perhaps many do without my seeing them. I do see a mailman occasionally struggling along. There was a time when I used to wait for him every morning. Not now. I also see stray dogs occasionally sniffing about. I flatter myself that they try to amuse me by their antics. In vain. Sometimes I hear the wails of an ambulance. And rejoice that yet another wretch has left this world or is about to. Even without snow, this street is seldom busy. Thank God! Otherwise my death would have been even more difficult. When there is no snow I do, occasionally, hear a few anonymous and lost birds. Calling each to each. With a pathetic insistence. Sometimes I feel happy because I think they are not calling me. Sometimes I feel happy because I think they are calling only, or also, me. The crow is my favourite bird. It is rather rare in these parts. The crow is known for its relentlessness. It expresses all its anguish through the same caw. It reacts to every outrage in the same voice—black and cruel—that tears away all one's masks and melodies without any pity. But, alas, I hear the crow only in my memory. Sometimes before dawn I try to reproduce its cries. There is no one to comment on the quality of my mimicry. Next to the crow I like the owl. The owl, too, is rare in these parts. Once upon a time, in one of these rooms, I had a wooden owl. I don't know what has happened to it. Sometimes I drop everything else and start dragging myself about, upstairs and downstairs, in search of it. And then I get so absorbed that I forget what I am looking for. Sometimes, late at night, I try to hoot like an owl. But there is no one to comment on the quality of my mimicry.

Apart from the birds on the other side of the street, where there are no houses now—perhaps there never were—there are some bare elms that are dying very fast. I anticipate they will die before I do. When one is just about to fall, a few tree-cutters come from nowhere and cut it down. Whenever they do I watch them from this window as they cut the diseased tree down and cart it away. It is quite likely that other old people also watch this operation from behind their windows. It is quite likely they do not. It is quite likely they are blind and have to be content with having all their fun through other faculties. It is quite likely they are deaf. It is quite likely they are both deaf and blind, in which case they do not even know what fun they are missing.

I should be ashamed of myself—I am—that even at my age I am fond of having fun. I should also feel pleased—I am—that even at my age I am fond of having it. Otherwise it would have been more difficult to pass the time. Of course, it wouldn't have been impossible even then. One of the complaints my friend, or foe, or visitor, or devil, has against me is that I am still fond of having fun. Which is why he has launched his campaign to uproot me from here, so that he can plant me at the edge of a deserted road, where I'll have no fun to beguile myself with. Even if he succeeds in his campaign, I am sure I will manage to find some fun even on the edge of that deserted road. There is no limit to my resourcefulness.

Across the trees on the other side of the street there is a jungle about which I know nothing. Sometimes I have an urge to run out of this house and take refuge in that jungle. This urge too might have been planted in my mind by him. Which is why I am afraid it will bear bitter fruit some day. It is quite likely that that deserted road he raves about is somewhere on the other side of that jungle. It is quite likely that some day I'll succumb to his suggestions and find myself moaning on the edge of that deserted road. But I'll not be able to move from here only because of his promptings. I'll have to consider my feeble body. Of course, he will say—he does—that bodily feebleness is no hindrance, because, according to him, standing on the edge of that deserted road, like a hunchback, and moaning, doesn't require any energy but will-power. He will say—he does—that dragging myself about in this house, upstairs and downstairs, not to speak of filling these notebooks, needs more energy. He will say—he does—that the energy I'll consume in standing and moaning, on the edge of that deserted road, will be more than replaced by the energy I will gain by standing still in the open air. He has always beaten me in argument. I hesitate to argue with him even in his absence. I'll see what happens. If he continues to pester me, I'll have to give up this house. Just as I did several previous places of refuge. Ultimately I will end by doing what he wants me to do. Just as I did several times before.

Dying Alone

No, I haven't forgotten that limousine. I have seen few cars as black and sleek as that. When for quite some time no one came out of it, I thought they might have made a mistake, and were feeling too embarrassed to correct it readily. I don't know why I assumed that there would be two of them in the car, both tall and dressed in ceremonial black. From my window all I could see was the car. If I could, I would have put my head out and asked who they were looking for. Or perhaps I'd have only put my head out so that they could see me and, in case they wanted to, ask me what I wanted to know. Perhaps I wouldn't have put my head out, even if I could, lest they should see me and start asking me questions. Meanwhile the car was getting more black and more sleek, even though, logically, it should have gotten less so. Perhaps it was thanks to this that I concluded the limousine was a hearse.

The first really tough question that arose in my mind then was this: How did the Funeral Home people know of the old woman's demise? I pondered this for a long time. I even considered the possibility that I might have informed them in some spell of unawareness. After staring at the phone for a while I came to the conclusion that, in view of the undisturbed layer of dust on the instrument, I couldn't have been the informer. Besides, I didn't know the number and name of any Funeral Home and the phone book was nowhere near the phone. Besides, I didn't even know that the old woman had died, if at all she had. Besides, had I known I wouldn't have called anyone else. I would have managed somehow to get over to her house. In which case I would have been standing or sitting by her dead body, thinking of my own death, or of my tumultuous affair with her, or shaking with the fearful hope that she would get up and say: Marry me! I looked around several times and was convinced I wasn't in her house. Now, if I hadn't sent for that limousine, who had? Could the old woman's neighbour on the other side have? Which would mean that the old woman had spent her last days in the lap, or at least the confidence, of that fellow, if he was a fellow. Then I put this possibility to sleep. Otherwise I would have either fainted or felt too angry to do anything. Then I thought that maybe the old woman herself had called them immediately before expiring. This possibility was no less acceptable to me. If she knew she was about to die and had some sense or strength left to call someone, why hadn't she called me? Because, after all, I had been the partner of her last ecstasies. After deriving sufficient distress from it, I rejected this idea also. It was riddled with flaws. The old woman, or any other ordinary person, cannot possibly have enough presence of mind, just before her end, to call a Funeral Home. Then I thought the old woman might have been connected with a Funeral Home through some electronic device. And as soon as she started breathing her last a bell had rung in the emergency room of the Funeral Home and they had rushed the limousine over.

Nobody had come out of the hearse yet. Did they expect the old woman to walk out of the house by herself? Then I thought perhaps the Funeral Home had been excessively precautious. In that case the men in the car must have brought popcorn and papers to amuse themselves while they waited. Their car, as big as a house, might even be equipped with toilet facilities. I had a great desire to rush downstairs and pass the time of the day talking with those men. Of course, I hadn't seen them yet. I wanted to ask them if they had come on their own or had been called by the old woman or someone else. I also wanted to know what the whole pre-arrangement had cost her, whether I could make a similar arrangement for myself, whether I could be of any help, whether the old woman was going to be cremated or buried. There were numerous other matters I wanted to ask them about. But, by the time I would get out of the house, they would be gone. If not back to the Funeral Home, at least into the old woman's house. In which case I would have to decide whether I should wait for them near the hearse or go in. I would perhaps decide to go into the old woman's house and tell them: I wish to claim this dead body; I was her last lover; but for my refusal to marry her I would have been her husband too; so her last rites will be presided over by me. I visualized their astonishment at my announcement. This delighted me so much that I had to close my eyes. Just as women have to while kissing or screaming with pleasure. Now, whenever I close my eyes, for whatever reason, I cannot open them again very easily.

Dying Alone

Sometimes it takes me so long to do so that I forget why I had closed them. I didn't forget this time even though it must have taken me long enough to open them again.

I noticed that one of the hearse's doors was open. And those two—I was amazed to see that my guess about their number, height, and dress had turned out right—stood a few paces away from the car. They had their arms folded across their chests and their heels raised. It seemed they were standing on their toes to peer into each other's eyes or play some other childish game. Their faces were brick red, their bodies wooden. Even as I watched them, they started nodding their heads—furiously. Then one of them put his hand, I don't remember whether it was the right or the left, on the other's shoulder, and both of them abruptly stopped nodding their heads. At that point one man's head was raised to the sky, the other's was facing the earth. I was curious about their next move. Then one of them pointed his thumb towards my window and said something to the other who shook his head. They were presumably talking about me. It was long since I had seen anyone talking about me. I felt grossly flattered. I had an urge to shout through the closed window: What is it that you want to know about me? Just then they bent their heads and started drawing lines with their toes. As if they knew I was at my window watching them. Then they resumed nodding their heads. Then they started sawing the air. My curiosity was killing me. My body behaved like an irritated insect's. I wanted to break the window and jump. I wanted to ask them what they had said about me to each other. If they said they were talking about the old woman, I wanted to ask them why one of them had pointed his thumb at my window. I seemed prepared to satisfy my curiosity at the cost of my life. It was long since I had been seized with curiosity. I had forgotten how foolish and reckless I always became when I was curious.

So I started dragging myself toward the door. I wanted to rush downstairs and out of the house. But the stairs have always been my bane. I have had numerous falls going upstairs or downstairs. Which is why, for days on end, if I am upstairs, I don't go downstairs and vice versa. I prefer the upstairs to downstairs. I have my provisions conveniently scattered all over the house, upstairs and downstairs. I don't need much to nourish myself—cereal, soup, and skimmed milk. All mixed together. I cannot digest anything else. Not that I can digest these. I do not have fixed hours for meals. I eat many times a day, at different times everyday. Regardless of appetite. Just as smokers smoke. Sometimes, in order to improve the taste, I add a drop of brandy to my formula. It makes it more nauseating. An occasional fit of nausea is good for my digestion. Also a necessary restraint on my need to eat. But the pretence of putting restraints on my needs is a mockery of my old age. For what can need make me do at my age! I feel depressed all of a sudden, I feel like beating my forehead. Fortunately my hands don't obey me any more.

Anyway. If I ever leave this house and, acting upon his orders, go stand on the edge of the deserted road he raves about, I will take a huge jar of my formula with me. He will be happy to hear this. He will say: I knew you wouldn't be able to resist my suggestion. After I am gone, my readers will benefit from my recipe for reducing the need for nourishment. I think I should write it down clearly and unironically: Mix cereal and soup and skimmed milk in equal portions; add twenty drops of brandy for every ounce of the other ingredients; drink a glassful down, keeping your eyes wide open, at one draught; keep drinking it every other hour until it threatens to come out of your nose and ears; if even after five doses you see no abatement in your need for nourishment, you'll have to accept you are irredeemable. This recipe is effective only if it is followed in good faith. The dosage has to be repeated at regular intervals. It doesn't guarantee anything more than a reduction of one's need for nourishment and allied hungers. Besides, since this need is closely connected with age, sex, weight, climate, culture, and similar other particulars of the person concerned, appropriate modifications of the recipe are absolutely essential. For instance, if the person belongs to a poor country with a tropical climate, then cereal, soup and skimmed milk can be replaced by rice, mud and buttermilk, and brandy can be replaced by a drop or two of country liquor or some other native intoxicant. I could cite countless other variations if I had the patience. A word to the wise. Of course, some countries and cultures have perfected a cuisine the very thought of which is enough to kill all need for nourishment. And then there

Dying Alone

are those who are nauseated by the thought of any food. Such exceptional people don't need my formula. Obviously.

I was going downstairs, one slow step at a time, and was yearning for a sip of my formula. That was another reason why I repeatedly forgot why exactly I was going downstairs. After I had gone down half the stairs, I was done for. My head was humming like a top. I could see spots in front of my eyes. I had to sit in order to recover my wits as well as will. I placed my elbows on my knees and my head in my hands. My favourite posture. In which I forget quite often that I am alive. Or that I have a body. A hidden observer might have imagined I was beseeching God to be merciful. I was in no state to beseech anyone, much less God. A brief session with my miseries, in this posture, almost always helps me overcome my fatigue and fear. I feel liberated. The difference between upstairs and downstairs disappears. The eagerness to reach anywhere disappears. After a few minutes I begin to hum my favourite song. *There is none other!* At such moments I am not complaining about the absence of any other, nor suggesting to myself, or to anyone, that any other would have mended matters. I am singing a statement of fact. I am also offering myself a faint illusion of being self-sufficient.

After some time, I don't really know after how long, I found that my head was together again, and my eyes alert. I remembered why I was heading downward. I put my hands on my knees and ordered myself to get up. I repeated the order several times until the knees began to knock each other. I knew that if they continued to do that I wouldn't be able to resume my descent, nor would I be able to go back upstairs, nor to keep sitting right there. If I had a rosary with me I might have started rubbing it. And dozed off. And tumbled downstairs. The stairs are wooden and covered by a dusty rug. So the tumble wouldn't have hurt me. But I couldn't tumble with my eyes open. If I had pen and paper I would have continued to sit and doodle until some suitable alternative had struck me. Or perhaps I would have doodled myself into unawareness. Or perhaps I would have started recording this experience and got rid of the desire to go downstairs. If I had been attacked by an itch, I might have forgotten myself in enjoying it. Of course, mine is not the right age for pleasurable itches. You need a soft skin and hard nails to enjoy an itch. But a few parts of the body remain sensitive until the end and can be depended upon for an occasional sensation. I tried to provoke those parts. Finding them inert, I left them alone and started staring at the white wall of the stairwell. I have noticed that, if you keep staring at a wall, sooner or later you become oblivious of everything else but the wall, which sooner or later rewards you with a reflection or a fear or a writing that you desire or dread. Old-fashioned ceilings with beams also had this propensity. One doesn't see those ceilings very often over here. Walls are more or less the same everywhere. So I fixed my eyes on the wall opposite me. After some concentration I saw the distorted face of the old woman. I was so painfully reminded of my riotous past with her and of the purpose of my descent that I rose in defiance of my lazy body and started moving downstairs, a slow step at a time. I am ashamed to say that, after a little while, I again forgot why I was going downstairs.

Enough of this. I should not stretch it out any longer. Suffice it to record that, finally, after fairly superhuman efforts, I reached downstairs. Because for the past several weeks or months or whatever I had been upstairs, it took me some time to discover downstairs. Everything looked alien at first. But then gradually it recovered the film of familiarity. Both these first impressions were equally unpleasant. I had a great urge to turn and start crawling upstairs again. Fortunately my body refused to comply. Since I was so close to the front door I thought of opening it to see if there was any mail. It has been years since I wrote or received any letter, but whenever by chance I am close to the front door, I am seized by the urge to open it and see if I have any mail. The last letter I received was about the death of those two. Both of them had ended on the same day. First my mother. Then my father. After three hours. They had talked of me before the end. My mother had asked: Where is he? My father: Why isn't *he* here?

On reading that letter I had felt that two of my phantoms had finally disappeared. This was soon after I had entered the phase of semi-total detachment and isolation. I had disconnected myself from everything and taken refuge in this house. I still spent my nights in the jungle of my nightmares and days in the garden of my day-dreams. I used to keep a close record of my nights and days. Some remnants of those records are, perhaps, still scattered all over this house. Somebody is bound to discover them after my death. Then came that letter informing me of their death. Which marked the beginning of my almost total detachment and isolation. After that I never had any nightmares about them. Now, whenever I think of them, I feel I am thinking of myself. At my age I am indistinguishable in my mind from my father and mother. At their deaths they were as old as I am now. I have no other way of measuring my age.

Reaching the door was quite arduous. Opening it was even more so. As soon as I opened it a gust of wild wind assaulted me. Like a lurking lover or enemy. I am afraid of wild winds. Like every lightweight old man. Reflexively I closed the door just as I was about to lose my foothold. But that gust had already entered and embraced me. Had I not kept my wits and will about me and started panting as I leaned against the wall, I would have collapsed right there. And this account of my misery would have remained unattempted. It would be wrong to infer from this sentence that I want this account to reach anyone. Or that I imagine it will ever reach anyone. Or that I hope it will reach anywhere. The torment of the journey is its own reward. This cliché is aimed at consoling this tale, not its teller. My intention, of course, is to leave unambiguous instructions that these notebooks should be cremated along with my mortal ruins. But I doubt if my instructions will be carried out. Survivors' curiosities about survivors is insatiable. Whole libraries are cluttered with the literary remains of ordinary persons. Or with books based on those remains. That is another reason I am not being totally candid in these notebooks. I believe that nobody dances absolutely in the nude. Even when they are alone. The key word here is *absolutely*.

Anyway. I didn't collapse despite the wild wind. I did forget, however, for a while, why I had opened the door. And why I had closed it. The scratches on the palms of my hands suggested I must have opened it for an emergency. So I began to pull it open once again. Doors have always either resisted or ignored me. This second time the gust of wind was less wild. So I stuck my head out and turned it right and left. As if I was being regaled by glorious prospects on each side. On my left I saw the open mouth of the empty mailbox, on my right the closed door of the old woman. The mailbox brought to my mind my deceased parents and long-forgotten friends. The closed door of the old woman reminded me of her insatiable desires. My mouth drooped. Picture to yourself a dying old man with a drooping mouth. He is bald. He is toothless. He wears a torn buttonless shirt. He is naked below the waist. He will remind you of a starved beggar from a poor country.

I stood there for a long time. Thinking now of the old woman, now of my parents and friends. When I thought of the old woman, I saw a pale, wrinkled woman stretched out on a clean, white bed. When I thought of my parents and friends, I saw myself besieged by numerous ghosts. All pale and wrinkled. When my neck was about to fall off, I started to pull my head in, slowly and carefully. It was then that my eyes fell on the vacant spot occupied earlier by that sleek limousine and those tall men in black. I instantly remembered why I was where I was. I reasoned that, since I was half out of my door, I should, perhaps, drag myself somehow to the old woman's door and find out what the matter had been. Then I remembered I was naked below the waist. I felt like laughing at my plight but suppressed it out of fear of coughing. I was afraid that if I went back in to look for trousers, the impulse to drag myself out and investigate would die or wither away. I was afraid I would forget why I was looking for trousers. I was afraid I would forget whether I was looking for trousers, or for some other missing thing or thrill. I was afraid I wouldn't be able to decide whether I was really looking for something or only pretending to. I was afraid that if I succeeded in finding my trousers I would have to start looking for my shoes. The moment I thought of shoes, my spoilt feet shouted—No shoes, please! Had it been night, I might have stepped out barefoot and bare-legged. Lost in these thoughts, I started playing with myself and forgot that my flower was past responding to any foreplay.

I should have been convinced that the old woman was dead, that her dead body had been driven away by those two tall men in black. But I had no evidence other than that of my own eyes to prove that that black sleek limousine had been there. And it has been long since I have stopped trusting my eyes. Besides, I hadn't yet resolved in my mind who had sent or did send for that car. Besides, I wasn't sure whether those two tall men in black had picked up the dead body of the old woman, assuming that they had come or been sent for that purpose. For all I knew, the old woman had died ages ago, and instead of finding her dead body in her bed, all they had found was a skeleton. In which case those men might have gone back for further instructions. In fact, I wasn't sure of anything. Not even of what I would do once I became sure of anything. This final twist in my thinking, not to mention the slowly mounting fatigue of my slow descent, made me impotent with rage. And before I could control myself or be controlled by my impotence, I pulled the rest of my torso in and closed the door.

For a while I stood there, shaking, my forehead pressed against the closed door, unaware that I was standing there. I kept feeling that the whole house, in fact the whole universe, was shaking with me. But I was in no position to stand there for too long. My legs were getting more limp and my eyes more hazy every second. Had I been in some other part of the house, I would have stretched myself out on the floor to regain my powers. But I have always resisted the urge to lie down in the narrow hallway. Perhaps because of the fear that, if someone came down from upstairs or in from the outside, I would be in the way. There is no one else upstairs. No one has come in from the outside for aeons. That friend or foe of mine, who appears of an occasional evening, doesn't count. I was trying not to move away from the door because I was afraid I would again forget why I had come downstairs. I shouldn't have worried, though, because sooner or later I manage to remember whatever I forget.

Time had slipped off my mind in the meanwhile. I had a vague feeling that I had been standing there all my life. Along with the contradictory feeling that not more than a moment had passed since my arrival there. Had there been a hole or crack in the door, I might have lost myself in peeping through it at the desolation outside. I've always held that the desolation looked at through a hole or crack has a glory all its own. I have often imagined breathing my last while in the standing position. And wondered at the way my body would fall. And at the thud it would produce. My innermost desire, of course, is that I should keep standing, if not straight at least crookedly, even after I have breathed my last. That is why I want to breathe my last while standing close to a wall or a door or a tree, so that, instead of falling all the way, my forehead or back is able to lean against that wall or door or tree. In other words I want that in my last moments of misery I should have a support handy, so that, instead of falling, I should look as if I am only about to fall. It might have been because of the force of this desire that my legs began to look alive. They seemed willing to groan, once again, under the burden of my torso. I was pleasantly surprised. Ordinarily, they are too far gone to be concerned with the rest of my body. Ordinarily, they respond only to pain in parts that are called joints. Or to emergencies that require kneeling or running. Of course, they haven't had to contend with any such emergency for ages. During my ardours with the old woman, I had to bend them frequently. But on those occasions their pain was drowned in my pleasure. The pain I got from my bouts with the old woman will always reappear in my memory as delight. I don't need to be told I am deceiving myself. I am thankful I am not deceiving anyone else. I don't need to be told that this senile romanticism doesn't suit me, that, at my age, according to the norm, I should be dignified and detached. But I have spent a lot of my life in self-castigation without getting any merit out of it. I don't need to be told that I won't get any merit out of my senile self-deceptions either. I persist in self-deception only because I want to persist in living. As long as I can. Any way I can. I don't need to be told that I won't get any merit out of this persistence. But I want to keep persisting. Without any prop. Without any protector. I am not unaware of the possibility that, sooner or later,

Dying Alone

I'll get fed up with all of this. And instead of continuing to carp in this monster of a house I will renounce it and set out in search of a new void. Where I will stand. Perhaps under a tree. And start refining some new lament. It is obvious that the suggestion of that devil is alive in me like a buried seed.

I dozed off while thinking of my death and that devil. During the doze an old nightmare revisited me. The central character of that nightmare was an old child, looking like a withered flower in an untilled field. Above him the flaming heaven. Under him the fallow earth. At a short distance from him a crow, shredding the desolate silence with his cawing. All around him a dead hot odour. I saw myself in that old child. Then my doze must have snapped prematurely like a yawn. When I came to I saw that my forehead was still propped against the door. And underneath my eyes was seething darkness. My mind was like a broken cage and my body like a hungry wolf.

And then suddenly the house rocked as the phone sang! I wish it had. I might have died of shock. My phone has been dead for years. I don't know why I don't have it disconnected. Perhaps I am still secretly waiting for a ring.

I lifted my forehead with great difficulty and felt reassured by the lukewarm pain at the back of my neck. A little later I started inching backward.

I am suddenly weary of this narrative or whatever it is. I don't need to apologize for this weariness. Nor do I desire to. It is in such moments that this isolation strikes me as an absolute bitter blessing, and the secret desire for company a shameful vice. But before I end I want to record that the old woman is indeed dead. I don't know how or when I became convinced of it. I mean I know but am not in a mood to go into details. I am indeed so weary that I am in a mood to do nothing. Silence is the only way out of this swamp.

Four

An ancient record seems stuck in its refrain: *I will not remember the times gone by!* I wish I could sing that. My back is turned toward the gramophone and my eyes toward the dust of times gone by, which is mixed with the dust of the rugs in this house. Quite often when I can't or don't want to do anything else, I start beating these rugs and the times gone by with a stick. For days after, I keep rubbing and wiping my nose. It is quite likely that the record is stuck in my memory. I can turn around and see, but I am afraid my head will refuse to cooperate.

I haven't gone back up since the day I came down in pursuit of the possibility of the old woman's death. Every now and then I've been forgetting why I came downstairs, whether I am downstairs or upstairs, whether the old woman is dead or I am. When I can't think of anything, I lift my face upward and caw like a wounded crow. This is an old habit of mine. It is more a feat than a habit. Had it been merely habit, it would have left me by now. When I was a boy my friends used to mimic other birds, but I always did the crow. My throat became scratchy with the effort, but the satisfaction of

Dying Alone

being different seemed worth it. Since then this skill has stuck to me. Whenever I caw the times gone by come back to me. And I feel as if they had never gone.

The song is over. I still haven't decided whether the record was playing in my memory or on the gramophone. Now even if I do turn around I won't be able to say for sure. I have often thought of smashing this record against the wall. I am deterred by the knowledge that both this record and the wall will survive my smashing.

What to do now? This question has been killing me all my life. Or at least so it thinks. Shall I dig up the times gone by or keep getting disgusted with those that are passing now? If I can try I can be disgusted by both simultaneously. But I will not try. I gave up trying ages ago. Ever since I took refuge in this house. I am exaggerating of course. I will spend the rest of my time without effort and desire. But since I am human, I can't vouch for myself. I can fall prey to any fear or temptation any time; I can be duped by any devil or desire any time. I think I should move a little further away from the gramophone so that I'm not tempted to play this record again. But before starting to move I should collect the droppings all around me. Some of these I will string into new rosaries; the rest I'll store in a jar. It is difficult to deduce from the dryness or the number of these droppings how long I have sat here. I have lost track of time. Thank God! These droppings do not smell. Thank God! It is not that I cannot smell anything. Even though my other senses have gone weak, the sense of smell is as strong as ever. For this also I am thankful. I notice that I have begun to regard all afflictions as blessings. This is not a good sign. It is not bad either. It is in between. Like all the other signs. Thank God again! I notice that this exclamation fits everywhere. In fact I am fast reaching a state where every exclamation fits everywhere. There is no such state. Thank God!

My droppings do not smell. If they had, I would have been dead of their odour by now. A hidden observer would imagine I am a decrepit keeper of a billy goat. Once, when I showed some selected smooth specimens to the old woman, she was so taken by them that she wanted to know if they were real pearls. I was bewitched by her innocence. I felt like telling her that they were aphrodisiac pills. I wish I had told her that. Anyway. I use them mostly for making my rosaries. Had I not severed all connection with the outside world, I would have used my rosaries as Christmas gifts. Now they serve as decorations for my house and stimulants for my hands. Sometimes, instead of rubbing them, I smell them out of habit, but there is no smell. Perhaps it is a sign that I am no longer ordinary. Which is why I don't throw them away. The ones I cannot use as rosaries I save in two blue jars. There is one upstairs and one downstairs. I have to be careful because they look very similar to the pills I take for indigestion. I don't know why I can't stop being careful. By now I should have reached a point far beyond discriminating between dung and dahlias. My regret should be that, when I should have been indifferent to filth, in my youth, I was so queasy.

Anyway. Before starting to drag myself away I collected all the droppings within my reach into a little heap. After this heap has become a little larger, I'll start pushing it toward the blue jar. Which looks more like a pitcher than a jar. Made by a master potter, it was always admired by my guests when I still had them. They wanted to know where I had bought or pinched it from. I used to tease them with an enigmatic smile. Actually, this jar, unlike the one upstairs, is my own creation. No one knows I have this skill. Just as no one knows the use to which I put it now. The jar upstairs was presented to me by a friend. I don't remember his face or name. I'll praise the upstairs jar when I go upstairs, if I do.

If I had read about two jars full of human droppings in a story or a novel, I would most certainly have taken them as symbolic.

Dying Alone

So the old woman is no more. I didn't go to her funeral. Because I never came to know of it. No one thought of inviting me. They might have thought I was dead. Or that I would be offended by the invitation. It is quite unlikely that anyone knew the old woman had been my lover, and would have been my wife but for my faint heart. Thank God for their ignorance! Otherwise they wouldn't have left me alone, to die in peace in this house. They might even have driven me out of it. I wouldn't have attended her funeral even if they had invited me. I don't have the right clothes. They wouldn't have let me in without them. Sometimes I amuse myself by imagining their shock. If I had shown up at the funeral in this shirt, bare below the waist, perhaps they would have pretended I wasn't there. Or remonstrated with me. Or beaten me away. It amuses me to imagine that they could have beaten me to death. Which would have been blamed on the alien bastards. And my soul—or whatever survives the body, if anything does—would have joined the old woman's. There was a time when I used to worry about soul and oversoul. Along with other enigmas.

So I never attended her funeral. Nor did I watch it from my window. But it pleases me to pretend that when they carried her to that sleek black limousine, I was at my window, watching them. By the time I am close to my own death, this pretence will have been transformed into a conviction. I will start believing that the old woman died in my arms. And her funeral was arranged and attended by no one except me. This hangs on the provision that I am still far from my end. A lot of time is required to transform a piece of fiction into fact.

The old woman's house remained vacant for I don't know how many weeks or months after her death. Now it is occupied by a few nuns. If not in fact, at least in my fiction. I haven't seen any face to face yet. Had I been upstairs, I might have succeeded in snatching a glimpse of one or some of them. One reason I haven't gone upstairs is that I have been hoping against all probability that one of these days one of them, perhaps their Mother Superior, will appear at my front door. I don't know in which corner of the house I will be when she rings the bell. She will be a picture of patience and peace while she waits for me. If I am upstairs, she may lose her patience and leave before my descent, which would be at one slow step at a time. And I wouldn't be able to decide for ages after whether that ring was real or imaginary. But, if I am downstairs, I'll manage to reach the front door before she leaves. Imagine then that I have opened the front door—to a smiling young or middle-aged or old nun. Her eyes are full of a messianic motherliness. I can't imagine the change in her on seeing me. I try to put myself in her shoes and her habit, and her in my bare feet and shirt. But I draw little more than a blank. It is not easy to discard one's body—and the point of view that comes with it. If her first glance falls on my face, she is likely to take me as an aged alien Christ. Or at least an avatar of one. This thought thrills me a lot. Christ and the Buddha have been my ideals for ages now. In my youth I doted on the dark blue Krishna. If her glance falls below my face, her eyes will close, leaving her mouth open. After sweeping her body with my eyes from head to foot and from foot to head, I will say: I am old but still redeemable. She will, however, remain convinced that I am unredeemable but not old. I can't go beyond this point. Even in my imagination.

I am suddenly sick of all this nonsense. Had there been an other around, I would have put my head on his shoulder and cried: For what unknown sins am I being punished! Or I would have stood before him and started to cough. And continued to cough until my last breath. Or I would have started to pummel him. Or I would have requested him to pummel me. But there is none other! Thank God! Even that mortal enemy of mine hasn't visited me for quite some time. He never does when I need him most. But there is no need to be angry. I am beyond anger. Or at least I should be. I am sure I'll survive this fit. As I have many others. There is nothing I cannot survive. Short of death I have endured everything. Short of death, nothing can destroy me now. The thought of death has chased my anger away.

Dying Alone

So I want to put a luminous nun in the old woman's place. Let me see. Why don't I dress up some day and knock at the doorstep of the imaginary nuns, on my knees, and implore them: I am your poor next-door neighbour; a friend, no, a lover, of the poor old woman who is no more; I am lonely now that she is gone; I have no one here to call my own; I have no one anywhere to call my own; I was born alien; I haven't been properly understood by anyone so far, not even by my fond old woman who is no more; otherwise she wouldn't have proposed to me; yes, it was her premature proposal that ended our affair; which is why I didn't learn of her death until it was too late; and now she doesn't let me die in peace; she visits me in various ghostly disguises; she insists I visit you and sing my hymns to her; which is why, my holy sisters, I am here, on my knees; please let me in, so that I can relate the story of my story and persuade one of you, perhaps, to take her empty place; if you don't take pity on me, I'll break my head against your doorstep; the country where I was born and burnt has a long and lovely tradition of supplicants breaking their heads against unresponsive doorsteps; if you don't want to hear about her, maybe you'd like to hear my moans about my old country; she too is like an old beloved to me; please don't blush, my holy sisters; meditate on my metaphor; take pity on my condition; see the suffering beneath my self-mockery; I beseech you; you may not see in me the Lazarus you know, but believe that I am no better than that lucky leper; at least tell me whether you see me or not; if you do, please raise me with your lily-white hands; true, I don't have the faith you do; but then I don't have any; which is why I am in this condition; which is why you shouldn't turn me away; I am not suggesting that you break your vows or anything; all I seek is compassion; all I need is compassion from one of you, from any one of you; you may have seen that I do not have much longer to suffer; that I am not too far from that afterworld in which I do not believe but you do; so, my holy sisters, preach to me the message of Christ; for all you know, some word or touch of yours may win me to your fold even now; please ignore everything I have said and raise me to your bosoms; **convince me of the ministry of Christ; at least say something, my** holy sisters, for I can't say much more; I am utterly lost; please find me; or ask someone else to; or. . . .

I have been drained—of everything—for the time being.

Five

Here I am, back again with this story. If it is a story; if I am here. In between I spent myself trying to take my other stories a little further. There is no dearth of incomplete stories in this monster of a house. They are scattered all over. Upstairs and downstairs. Like my droppings and rosaries. I scattered them, designedly, so that at least one of them is within my reach wherever I unfortunately happen to be.

It has been long since I sat squarely on both buttocks. Like a normal human being. All I have now by way of buttocks is a few rags of flesh swinging from my hip bones. When I sit I feel I am sitting on somebody's wrinkled breasts. Which is why I sit gingerly whenever I do, which is not too often. Ordinarily, I either crawl or pace as worst I can. One incidental advantage of crawling and pacing is that I am saved from the temptation and torment of writing. Writing should no longer be a temptation for me, but it is, perhaps because of the torment that it also is. I can say, if I want to, in the manner of some I remember, that writing is my rock. But I can't in all honesty say it. Even if I want to, which I don't. Life itself is my real rock. This sentence has brought back to my mind several old sinners who used to resort to similar sentences when caught in corners.

Anyway. I can't really justify my numerous narratives. In the beginning I was convinced I meant them to be for my eyes only. I was determined to burn them before my banishment from here. I am still, but I see a crack in my determination now. It has been caused by several factors. One of them is that I have gradually, and involuntarily, fallen in love with my words. Which doesn't make the thought of burning them thrill me any more. All it does is produce a dry dread. In the beginning it afforded me the courage to let myself go. By the beginning I mean the phase immediately following my confinement to this house. Those early outpourings are also scattered all over. Upstairs and downstairs. If I really want to burn them before my end, I have to start gathering them now. But there is no guarantee that I won't be surprised by my end before I have finished gathering them. Realistically speaking, it will be difficult to burn the entire heap even if I am able to gather all of them before the end, even if I'm not surprised by it. Some of it will survive, half-burnt or unburnt, enough to arouse erroneous notions about me and my lifelong labours. I shouldn't worry about them but I do. Which is why I keep inventing excuses. Otherwise I would have stopped writing and started gathering all that lies scattered all over, upstairs and downstairs, so that I can be reasonably sure of having done my best to find everything I could burn. I have to admit I won't be able to burn with my own hands what my hands have produced. But why worry! The worst that can happen will be that whosoever reads my laments will admire me, marvel at my will, and wonder why I worked without any reward until the end. It is also likely that soon after my death this house will be put to auction, along with its contents. And its new owner will have it demolished. Or at least have all its contents, rosaries as well as notebooks, thrown on the town dump. But even then the possibility, howsoever faint, of the survival of some of these notebooks, and of their being read and condemned, remains.

Dying Alone

To tell the truth, I am looking forward to posthumous fame. That's why I won't get any. I may not, but I am looking forward to it. Sometimes I have played with the idea that I should spread a rumour I am dead and hide and see what happens. I am afraid nothing will. Every ordinary person has played with some such idea at some time or the other. Which is why we have ghosts and gnomes. But where will I hide myself? The moment I get out of this house, I won't know what to do or where to go. It is quite unlikely that I'll ever enter a phase, before the end, in which this house will cease to have any hold on me. That I'll ever renounce it for the edge of a deserted road. And devote myself entirely to moaning in measure. Not in order to arouse anyone's compassion. Nor in order to appease or entertain him. But for its own sake. For all I know he is already waiting somewhere on that barren road for me. Let him. For the time being I am content to remain here in this house. And suffer in my own insufficient way. I would like to imagine that every old person of my age is deranged by similar delusions. Not every old person but every old exile. Does it mean that even at my extremity I am not rid of the rigours of exile? I am not going to devote this notebook to those rigours. I better confine it to an account of my various bodily botches. This decision to record various woes in separate notebooks is yet another indication of my desire that this mess should not only survive me, but also offer instruction and delight to the coming generations. Not to mention my desire that it should establish me as a voracious woe-monger.

It is obvious that I'll never be able to burn my notebooks. Which is another reason why I want to take one of my imaginary new next-door neighbours into my confidence. So that, after I am no more, she is able to dispatch all or some of these notebooks to a library in my native land, along with a long covering letter mentioning that this was my last wish; and that these notebooks contain the essence of my experience; and that no one understands my language in this country; and that few will understand my language even in my own country; and that, taking into account the last will and testament of an aged exile, etc.

This strange idea occurred to me only a while before. Which is why it seems so simple. I'll complicate it later. Maybe I'll start corresponding with a librarian experienced in the upkeep of odd collections instead of leaving it to an innocent nun. I wish I still had a dependable friend over there. For all I know, all my friends have died. If a few tough survivors are still there, I don't know their whereabouts. Even if I did, I wouldn't dare to contact them. Even if I did, I wouldn't get a straightforward answer. I don't think I can correspond with my compatriots without unpleasant consequences. I am afraid I have forgotten the customs of my country. In fact, the chances of my papers being accepted by a library over there will be better if someone else represents me after I am dead. After being accepted they will perhaps be left to rot in a dingy damp room. I don't think anybody over there will be keen or curious about them. I don't think anybody over there is keen or curious about anything. It is quite likely that everything has changed for the better or the worse since my banishment. I had better squelch this snake of thought right here. Even if some angry seeker after my anonymity happened to see any of my notebooks, he would be convinced, after turning a page or two, that it was all incoherent. After which he would either cast the thing aside and resume his daily death, or start a campaign for immersing my notebooks in one of the annual floods that I am sure still ravage my country.

So, once again, I am back with the thought that I should try to burn everything while I am still half alive. I'll let this thought throb a while in my inner darkness.

I went back a few pages and discovered I was bemoaning my inability to sit squarely on my buttocks. But, of course, I do sit somehow every now and then. I am always bare below the waist. As I have boasted several times before. There are many reasons for this. As I might have mentioned before. The bones of my buttocks have gone soft now. Had they been hard and inflexible, like real bones, I might have had to spend the rest of my life standing. Then I wouldn't have had the sores I do. One reason I am naked below the waist is these sores. So that, even when I sit, I am an inch or so above ground. One reason for this, of course, is that I am practically

Dying Alone

weightless now. I could compare myself to a sparrow, but I do, actually, to an old eagle. I have to stop and laugh.

I think I was unconscious for a while. Or perhaps for a few days. I don't know how I came to. Nor why I became unconscious. It is quite likely that what I am raising to the status of unconsciousness was no more than a swoon or a spell of sleep. Had I not broken all my watches and clocks—not that I had too many of them—long ago, in a fit of fury, caused by something I don't remember, and taken a pledge not to consult a calendar or radio, I wouldn't be in this timeless state now. Of course, I can call the operator for time and weather, but I won't. I could even buy a new watch, but I won't. I think it is far more interesting to make your own more or less wrong guesses about the time instead of having accurate secondhand information about it. Of course, it is even more interesting to be free of the necessity of knowing time. In fact it is so interesting that interesting is not the word. I haven't yet attained that freedom. I have occasionally cherished the delusion that I have. But if I truly had, I wouldn't have bothered to know whether I was unconscious or ill, or just asleep for a while or for a few days. This obsession with time also proves that I am of dust dusty. If any proof was needed. The desire to rise above my dust also proves that I am of dust dusty. If any proof was needed. Dust has its own fragrance. You can't get rid of it by calling it ordinary.

Even if, in fact, I didn't lose consciousness, I want to proceed on the assumption that I did, in effect, lose it. For a while. This arbitrary assumption will, I hope, help me to proceed. I can no longer bear the distance between the pen in my hand and the blank paper before me. I believe that every old man, who has reached a certain age and a certain degree of despair, should be provided with a pitcher of black ink and a sheaf of blank paper. Along with a room and an atmosphere appropriate to his angst. So that he can keep a record of his dying. After his death his record should be submitted to a respectful scrutiny. Preferably under the supervision of men who have arrived. Will my record be treated to such a scrutiny? What will happen to it if it is not? These are the questions that often drive me crazy. And suggest that I should burn everything before I die. Apparently, I can't help nursing the delusion that my notebooks contain numerous hopeless messages for the coming generations. If I do not stop doing it, it is bound to bloom into a belief. Then I won't be able to die in peace, because my eyes will remain fixed on my notebooks until my end; and I shall keep looking for a reliable heir, who will take over my dedication to them after I am gone. Next time that devil visits me I will try to drag him into the future of my notebooks. He won't take me seriously. He has never taken these notebooks seriously. He regards them as the fruits of my idleness. He believes I would have attained authentic non-attachment but for my addiction to these notebooks. I don't know why the bastard has always been bent upon making me non-attached. If he has his way, these notebooks will be destroyed. Which is another reason I don't want them to be destroyed after I am gone. And certainly not by him. But his end will probably precede or coincide with mine. No, on second thoughts, I will not consult him about this matter. He won't offer any sound suggestions. Perhaps he will start tearing me apart for wanting to survive my death. It has been long since his last visit. I have begun to hope that I am rid of him forever. Which means he will reappear one of these days.

I can probably estimate the duration of my unconsciousness, or whatever it was, from the quantity and quality of the droppings around me. I have often deduced duration from similar statistics. But I am not sure whether, just before my spell, I was sitting at this spot or some other spot, whether I was absorbed in my memoirs or some other nonsense, whether I was surrounded by my droppings or only drops, and so on. I don't have enough hard evidence to go on. My estimate is likely to be erroneous. Besides, I can't be sure that all these droppings are entirely mine. A rat might have added his own to the pile. But I doubt it. There are no rats in this house. Or else they would have nibbled me and my notebooks into nothing by now. No, there are no rats in this house, nor any bats. To an infant, I myself would be no more than a rat or a bat. In my sleep, I sometimes see myself as either or both—probably under the subliminal influence of a well-known masterpiece read ages ago.

After making numerous errors in counting these droppings, I have settled for an incorrect figure. On the basis of this figure, and the texture of this stuff, I have concluded I must have been out for no more than three or four weeks. I am disappointed. I had hoped I would conclude I had been out for at least a few months. I even wanted to think that, after that unconsciousness, or perhaps because of it, I would find I had been rejuvenated. It is quite likely my speculation is inspired by my desire to delude my body. It is too late to draw a line between my consciousness and unconsciousness. Hence I am discontinuing this train of thought right here. I will concentrate on the passing moment instead.

At this moment, then, I am busy writing this. With my face turned half toward the door and half toward this notebook. It may not be exactly half and half though. There was a time, in an effort to be absolutely faithful to reality, my sentences used to somersault before collapsing. Now I don't have that kind of patience. Now I settle for a semblance of absolute exactitude. My knees are looking up to my face. I am sitting on the rug. The rug has many faded colours. I am bare as usual below the waist. And dripping as usual. Which explains the faint odour in the air. The air itself is faint. Around me there are three small piles of my droppings. Making me look like an old peddler of dried berries. Waiting for customers. About to explode. This analogy has startled me with a nightmarish recollection of a crowd of old berry-peddlers. At a few paces from me there is a dead gramophone. Around it there are a few heart-breaking records. All of them variously chipped. Whenever I play them, mostly in my imagination, I feel I am listening to a parrot. A pin does duty for the needle. I don't know what I will do when this pin wears out or is lost. These records still have it in them to choke me with lumps. I don't hear their scratches. Their sound is painful enough to drive my senses away. When they return I feel like a fool hanging from his heels, from the top of a mountain.

Of course, I am exaggerating. I wanted to heap scorn on my sentimentality, using these records as an excuse. They do not do anything to me any more. They produce a sound similar to my own voice. While listening to them I feel I am singing a swan song to myself. I shouldn't shed tears over my own swan song. I don't. All I do is laugh. But my laughter is more mirthless than ever. This too is an exaggeration of a half-truth. It is too late to make an odious comparison between tears and laughter.

Apart from those three piles of droppings, there are numerous half-read, ill-read, and unread books lying around me. Looking like little corpses. If a stranger were to come in, he would take me for a decrepit but tenacious scholar, lost in his definitive researches. To tell the truth, I don't do anything but kick these books around. When I am too far gone to do that, I gaze at them in disbelief. And in utter contempt. Not because these books have done me any harm. Or misguided me. Or prevented me from any action or inaction. I can't accuse them, in good conscience, of being boring or banal. Not because they are not. I can't even accuse them, in good conscience, of being irrelevant or unnecessary. Again, not because they are not. There was a phase when I was obsessed by the need to know which book is deep, and how deep, which word is right, and how right, which sentence is strong, and how strong, and so on. I shouldn't let myself go on about this ancient obsession. Now these books are no more than the motes in my eye, which I can neither eject nor ignore. They lie scattered all over the place. Upstairs and downstairs. Most of them look lousy, thanks to the maltreatment I have given them. If that stranger, mentioned above, were to come in, he would imagine I am a book-hating bull. I am not a book-hater. Even now, sometimes, quite unaccountably, I am so fascinated by a book that I feel like dropping everything and starting to chew it. But soon enough this fascination is ousted by my indifference. A few make me wish I had written them. But soon enough this wish is scorched by my scorn. Thank God! There was a phase when I used to be ravaged by the desire to overshadow the literary world. Like a bloody sky. My addiction to these notebooks is a kind of perverse penance for that desire. I can't say, but I'd like to think it is primarily to pass the time. So that I can keep myself to myself. So that I can avoid other inanities. While waiting for the end. Even that self-appointed guardian of mine doesn't believe my main purpose in these, my literary, labours, is to pass the time while waiting for the end. Even I am not quite ready to believe myself.

Dying Alone

What then is the truth? He maintains I'll not arrive at any truth as long as I am in this house, wasting away in spreading ink on paper. He wants me to renounce everything and rush to some deserted road. And start staring at the nothing ahead of me and moaning ceaselessly. I maintain he is mad. But I'm not without a lurking doubt he may be right. Then I wonder why, at this extremity, should I bother to renounce anything? Why should I allow myself to be lured out of this house? Away from my rosaries and notebooks and books? I am quite content with this continuous carping. When it exceeds its limits, perhaps I shall be delivered from, or driven out of, this refuge. Then I will follow that swine. Into some new swamp. Or, improbably, into some new bliss.

Around me, apart from fallen books, there are a few faded pictures covering the various cracks and stains on the various walls. It has been long since I glanced at any of them. I am quite close to one of them though. I don't actually look even at this one, but I see it whenever I close my eyes. It represents an old cobbler, bent over an old boot. Its colours seem to have been mixed with blood and mud. Its lines drawn by nails. Its canvas made of a rare animal's hide. It often reminds me of an old friend of mine who gave it to me. I can't imagine the darkness he is in now. I am not prepared to imagine that he is dead and happy. In some mad moment, I imagine that he is eternally present in that picture. That he is watching me even as he sits crouched over that old boot. In some other mad moments I imagine that he has changed into the ruthless friend or foe who makes a clean sweep of all my hard-earned doubts whenever he visits me. Ages ago, while presenting this picture to me, his eyes devouring mine, my friend said in an extraordinarily soft but ominous voice: Don't you ever lose it! At that moment I had taken his injunction as a parody of all farewell ceremonies. His words, however, have been carved on my consciousness all these years. I have carried this picture all over the world. If I had come across this picture in a story, I would have searched it for the implications and intentions of the author. There was a phase when I used to be tormented by the implications and intentions of every author. It is quite likely that my friend meant to burden me with the task of interpreting this picture. It is quite likely that I am still engaged in that task. It is quite likely that, but for this picture, I wouldn't have been bent now over this notebook. Waiting for the next phase. It is quite likely that I am aping this old cobbler, that I will continue to bend over my boot until the end. If I had come across a similar critical interpretation of an image elsewhere, I would have been reduced to tears.

Apart from the pictures there are a few fine cobwebs all over the house. Made not by me but by a few master spiders. Out of my dirt of course. If that stranger, mentioned above, were to come in, he would compare me to a dying spider. An ordinary stranger wouldn't. Ordinary people use their imagination only when they are angry. The stranger I keep invoking has to be extraordinary. Why would an ordinary stranger come into this house in the first place? Why wouldn't he? Wasn't that old woman ordinary? Am I myself not? Isn't everybody? What is my measure anyway? There was a phase when I used to worry endlessly about whether I was ordinary like everybody else I knew. That worry, obviously, is still clinging to me. Otherwise I wouldn't be here. Whenever I am in this mood, and the ground seems to be slipping away from under me, I am suddenly visited by that mentor of mine. Twisting his lips into a smile, he says: If you want to become extraordinary, you will have to renounce your last refuge and follow me to that spot on the edge of that deserted road; once you are there you'll stop discriminating between pain and panacea, between ordinary and extraordinary, between anything and nothing; once you are there, if you are lucky, you'll have a glimpse of the great void you've been looking for all these years.

I've never been able to reproduce the sound of his speech precisely. Or to understand my reaction to it. Or to decide whether he is mocking me or making me aware of my destiny. Or to choose between following him to the edge of that deserted road and sticking to this refuge. I haven't been able to decide so far as to what he really wants. Or what I really do. Or whether he only wants to put my infirmity to an unnecessary test. I haven't been able to decide so far whether he is or not, whether I am or not. I am about to cross the bridge after which the difference between him and me will become negligible in my eyes. For a while longer, however, I want to linger on this side of that bridge. I wonder whether he feels any pity for me or only remorse, as he watches me from his point of vantage. I wonder whether he will come soon and try once again to subvert me or test me with his unpresence and silence. If any stranger, or the same I've invoked before, were to come in and read what I have just written, I doubt if he'd understand its purport. I am not sure whether I myself do.

I've got to interrupt myself, and attempt another take-off. Me and my take-offs! O you frequently invoked stranger, please burst into a laugh if you are anywhere around!

Suddenly the bell breaks into a ring. I am not startled because I can't be. Not the slightest sign of surprise or horror or happiness appears in my eyes or on my face or anywhere else. But this is unconvincing. It has been so long since I last heard the bell that, more likely than not, I'll jump out of my skin at the feeblest ring. Or at least those parts of my body that are not completely paralysed will come up with some sensation. Or perhaps those parts will go numb. The tinkle of a bell shouldn't be unfamiliar to me, to any part of my body. I have been all ears for it for ages now. I resorted to this exaggeration only in order to revive a dead phrase. Even so, I doubt if any other prisoner has ever waited as eagerly as I have for the ring of a bell or some similar other sound announcing an event. If elsewhere in this notebook, or in some other, I've bragged about being indifferent to bells or events, it was only to give myself courage to endure my isolation.

To cut this prevarication short, I don't think I will be unaffected by a sudden ring. Even if my body fails to react promptly, it is bound to tardily. By that time the visitor will have moved on to another bell, in order to ring it or to wonder whether he should. Jokes apart, I think that my mind, if not my body, will jump out of my skin at the sudden ring. Many conjectures will flash across it about the appearance and the reality of the ringer of the bell, about his intentions, about the first impression he will make on me and vice versa, about the disappointment that will follow the first impression, about our subsequent embarrassment. I will choose my conjectures according to the intensity of the ring. But this is madness. I won't make any conjecture, nor will it be necessary. As soon as I hear the ring, I shall shout: I'm coming, I'm coming. Let me imagine then that I have made this answer. I feel a little surprised at the loudness of my voice. I lower it as I answer once again: I'm coming. I'm coming! I sound like a feeble messiah assuring his followers about his intention to come eventually. I start crawling toward the front door, with an excruciating slowness. Because of holding the same posture, for I don't know how long, my limbs have lost all contact with one another. So with every little heave toward the door a groan escapes my lips. I don't want my visitor to overhear my groans. He might imagine I'm a monster. He might panic. The thought pleases me. I stop crawling in order to ask myself: What do you want? I am seized by a fit of laughter. I suppress it inhumanly and resume my crawl. Then I wonder why I am crawling, why I don't get up and walk. Inch by slow inch. I decide that the pace of my crawling is perhaps a little faster than that of my walking would be. Besides, I have begun to enjoy using my hands as my feet.

I can't help wondering about the identity of my caller as I crawl. I am sure it is not him. He never rings the bell. He knows the door is always open. Even if it were not, he has his own key. Even if he didn't, he'd able to break it open. I hope the caller is one of the next-door nuns. I hope she is sweet and tender. My snail's pace will drive her away, unless she is abnormally patient, by nature or nurture or by both. It is quite likely my caller is a visitor from abroad. He may even be from my old country. In which case his patience will be phenomenal. As I think of my country, my eyes are dimmed. Just then the ring is repeated. This time it is tender. As if it is asking me not to hurry. It seems to me that I have been crawling to the door for ages. Also that I'll be able to reach it only after ages of further crawling. Also that perhaps I'll soon forget why I am crawling toward the door. Also that I'll soon start crawling back to my starting point. Also that I'll forget why I am crawling back and start crawling back to the door. Meanwhile my caller will have walked away. Or he'll ring the bell again. And I'll have forgotten the earlier rings. I'll react differently this time. I may even start crawling upstairs. So now I am crawling and crying simultaneously: I'm coming, I'm coming, I'm coming.

By the time I reach the door, my hands are tired, my throat is dry, my trunk is torn. But my face is refulgent, with accomplishment, comparable to the moonshine in historic ruins, or to the flowers on the grave of an unknown other. How to end this imaginary journey to the front door? One way is to imagine that, on opening the door, I find nobody. And feel pleasure instead of dismay. Because the futile activity has helped me to pass the time, without my having to meet anyone. Also it will enable me to pass some more time. In going over the whole experience one more time: Did the bell really ring? Was someone there? Did he leave in impatience? Was his impatience justified? Was it a practical joker? Did the bell perhaps burst into a ring because of some inner upheaval? This end seems a dim derivation, from a novel that I read, or wrote, ages ago. Or was it a play? Or was it a poem? Or was it an essay? Another, somewhat commoner, end could be this: as soon as I open the door I die without knowing who the caller was. The best thing about this end is that I won't have to bother about the events subsequent to my end. Still another end would be to imagine that, as I open the door, I am greeted by a gorgeous nun. I look like an adder to her. I feel faintly ashamed. And faintly aroused. I don't want her eyes to fall on my ugly legs. I realize that, to her, I must look ugly all over. Particularly in this undignified posture. Even as I am girding up my loins to get up, she sits down and puts my head in her lap. I close my eyes. My face is radiant. My entire body is lit up. She cannot stand this splendour. She drops my head on the doorstep and runs out in fright. And then I hear his voice as he hisses: Would you like me to help you get up? Or would you like to tell me what you are doing here?

Six

I've decided to crawl upstairs, which is why, perhaps, I am here, in the narrow hallway, stretched out, close to the stairs. I am here, in the narrow hallway, stretched out, close to the stairs, which is why I think I have, perhaps, decided to crawl upstairs. Whether I've decided to or not, I am here, stretched out, close to the stairs. I have a notebook in my hands. Perhaps I am here because I wanted to open the front door. Perhaps I opened the front door and closed it when I saw the darkness standing outside. I shall reach upstairs sooner or later if I start crawling now. Even if I don't I'll have the satisfaction of having done my worst. But I needn't rush. I shouldn't take any new step, at this stage, without turning it over and over and viewing it from every side. This is the only advantage, if any, of this stage. The freedom to procrastinate. For my real aim now is not to arrive anywhere, but to have a premonition of the process and futility of arriving and of not arriving, anywhere. The freedom to end without illusions. But, had I really risen above all illusions, I wouldn't have even thought of crawling upstairs. I would have noticed no difference between upstairs and downstairs. This is the point *he* has been raising repeatedly of late: Since even this solitary confinement has failed to emancipate you

Dying Alone

from distinctions between upstairs and downstairs, I want to lure you to the edge of that deserted road, where you won't be beguiled by upstairs and downstairs, where you'll be able to moan without any distraction. He goes on to say: You haven't risen above illusions, which is why you keep pouring ink over paper, which is why I want to see you without your props. He says: You used to say that once your basic needs were met, you'd devote all your attention to attaining a state of trance, but I notice that you still keep casting about in search of this or that, you still keep hoping to hear from, or about, some visitor or the other, you still keep dreading your death, you still keep regurgitating your past lives, you still keep justifying yourself; which is why I want you to follow me to another level where you can create a new inferno for yourself. In spite of his exhortations I am still here. Whether he admits it or not, I think I have risen above the most deadly illusions. Otherwise I wouldn't be here, in this dead house, cut off from all ordinary connections. He says: This is the biggest illusion of all. Let him. I am getting eager for the boredom I'll experience upstairs. I've been downstairs so long that I have forgotten the devastating sights I used to see from the windows upstairs. I haven't really forgotten them. I am only deluding myself. I won't succeed in deluding myself. But I will pretend I have. And I shall be able to ride this pretence to the upstairs. And I'll wait for the next pretence. So that I can ride it downstairs.

The question may be raised.... Ah! This silly clause has revisited me after a long time! I shall punish it for its return by repeating it to death. Whenever an old forgotten clause or word or a metaphor recaptures my pen, while I am unguarded, I feel as if an old forgotten friend were trying to embrace me. I feel pleased as well as nauseated by this cloying fidelity. I cherish my lust for my language. People of my age generally feel compelled to cling to God. I'm clinging to my language. Even though my innermost desire still is to cling to nothing. Since I have this desire, I cannot free myself of desire. I am well aware of this tautology.

So, then, many questions may be raised: Why am I still stuck with this distinction between upstairs and downstairs? Even now when I am so close to the end? Why don't I devote the rest of my days to revisiting my past? Why am I not invoking some deity instead of yearning for a nun or nurse? Why am I not waiting for a miracle? Why am I pinned on the cross of fundamental questions, instead of trying to make a cross out of this superficial rhetoric? One infuriated answer to all these would be: These questions have been doing their ugly dance around me all my life while I've been trying to strip them bare of their confusions, and now, in this last lap of my anguish, I have decided to meet my end, with all my inconsistencies intact, without any loud claims about having attained enlightenment or liberation. In the process of bringing this sentence to an end, all my wrinkles have begun to dance, I can't say whether with delight or shame, perhaps only in order to suggest that, at my age, I shouldn't use 'dance' even as a metaphor.

The question may be raised: If it is accepted that life, for you, has been one unmitigated anguish, doesn't it become all the more imperative that your face should be radiant with it, like a faded moon, so that others should not presume to pity you? My answer would be: Imperative or not, this question reeks of hope, whereas my effort is to endure this final anguish without any hope of ending or overcoming it. This effort also reeks of hope. I'm aware of my fallacy.

The question may be raised: Wouldn't you agree that even your anguish is not endless, that, with your end, your anguish and your life also will end? My answer would be: Yes, but how does it reduce the intensity of my anguish, or the intensity of my dread of its end—of my death?

The question may be raised: Why don't you commit suicide then, in order to save yourself from this anguish and this dread? My answer would be: Suicide at my age would be like a joyless sin, or a post-coital kiss; hence I am determined now to hack it out, willy-nilly, till I die, for I've finally arrived at a point where life and death are one. This answer strikes even me as empty and unconvincing. But then every answer has always struck me as empty and unconvincing. Which is why I am here. Which is why I am nowhere.

The question may be raised: Are you grumbling or being grateful? My answer would be: I wish I knew but I think I am doing both; which is why I am here, in this house, which is why I am nowhere, even in this house; which is why I keep rubbing these rosaries; which is why I keep chanting 'There's none other'; which is why I keep hoping that someone will take me by surprise; which is why I want to stop hoping that someone will take me by surprise; I mean this is the sum total of my gain from my anguish, I mean the strength—ah—to endure this anguish, if this weakness can be called strength.

The question may be raised: Why do you plunge into solemnity at the mere mention of death or suicide? My answer would be: I have been immersed in solemnity all my life; which is why I am not drowned yet; which is why I am always drowned; which is why I believe I will surface sooner or later, unless I am utterly drowned before then, unless I am already utterly drowned.

The question may be raised: If this is the truth, why are you moaning? Why don't you suffer serenely, like other alienated old people of your age? Why are you bare below the waist? Why aren't you free from lust? Why don't you listen to yourself? Why, in short, this constant carping, this continuous seeking? My answer would be: I am different from other alienated old people of my age; or at least I think I am; I want to suffer according to my own system; I am bare below the waist so that I can drip without impediment, without having to change; I wish I could be free from lust; I wish I could listen to myself; I have to keep carping and seeking as long as I am here—if it can be called carping and seeking, even if it cannot be.

Now I'll pause a while and wait for my mouth to moisten. I lack the energy to reach for water. My energy is wayward. It disappears all of a sudden, and then it reappears also all of a sudden. I am waiting for its return.

So here I am at the foot of the stairs. I've always been particularly close to stairs. Just when I was about to crawl upstairs, I was inundated by questions. Even now, if one of my neighbours came in through the front door, I'd drop my decision to crawl upstairs. I am still smacking my lips in the hope of a little moisture. If I could stop writing for a while more and relax, with my back against the wall or my head on my knees, I might feel a little less dry. But relaxation in either of these postures has its own dangers. My neck may snap or sprain itself in such a way that it will become necessary to break it. Then, if someone rang the bell or just barged in, I'd reflexively give a start and break not only my neck but also my spine. And then there is the risk of falling soundly asleep. All discomforts other than those of my bed are more acceptable to my sleep. And then, if, on waking up, I find I've lost once again my reasons for being here, at the foot of these stairs, I'll have to start searching for them again. Above all I don't want to breathe my last here at the foot of the stairs. Relaxation, therefore, is ruled out. Of course, it will be vaguely, or perhaps, clearly, symbolic if I am found dead here at the foot of these stairs. But I'd prefer to die, if I have to, in that room upstairs. Which I've always regarded as the centre of my life in this house. Against those walls I've often knocked my head even as I was pouring my heart out to them. Through that rattling window I have feasted my eyes on so many scenes of the world outside: the desolate street, the stunted tree, snow, rain, birds, leaves, the lost ones. No, if I have to die in this house, I must in my moan-room upstairs. Bent over my desk. Ogling the vulgar woman on the cover of a Hindi magazine. One eye fixed on the emptiness outside the window, the other entangled in the endless darkness inside. Surrounded by my thirsty plants. Rubbing one of my choicest rosaries with one hand, stretching my saga with the other. Casting a curse over my life and work. Enough. Unless I want him to come in at this point. And start smiling. Like a snake. He considers my obsession with death either inane or romantic. He wants me to start a new life. On the edge of a deserted road. With my eyes fixed on the nothing ahead of me. And my back bent. I don't know why. When I ask him, he says: Follow me without a fear. I rejoin: How can I be sure you won't mislead me again, that you aren't yourself misled again. He answers: You can't be. I retort: Then why should I follow you? He retorts: Because I want you to. I can't but laugh at his presumption.

The question may be raised: What do you get in this house that you won't elsewhere? My answer would be: What will I get elsewhere that I don't in this house? The question may be raised: So you won't leave this house even for a spell? My answer would be: If the street is cleared of everybody, all windows are closed, everybody is ordered to go to sleep, or go blind, or at least be blindfolded for a while; if, in short, I can be assured that nobody will see me, I may be able to bring myself round to leaving this house and reeling about for a spell. The question may be raised: Do you really think your conditions could be met? My answer would be: No. The question may be raised: So you won't, under any condition, be willing to obey him and renounce this house in favour of that deserted road he has chosen for you? My answer would be: The decisive factor would not be my willingness but the strength and length of his insistence, because the truth is that I've always succumbed to him sooner or later, which is why I am here, which is why I am nowhere, which is why I have never been anywhere. The question may be raised: If this is the truth, then why are you trying to put it off; why don't you volunteer to renounce this house and follow him to wherever he wants to take you? My answer would be: Because I want him to shoulder the responsibility for all the consequences of my next move. The question may be raised: Does he have shoulders? My answer would be a silly and sour laugh.

My laughter has ended. I wish I too had, along with it. Then I could have boasted I died laughing. I haven't died yet, but I am afraid this laughter has wrought a few basic dislocations in my structure. It seems I have been literally bent double by it. If this turns out to be true, I am afraid I won't be able to resist my move to the next stage any longer. What happened was that my laughter collapsed, as usual, into my fit of coughing, and my fit of coughing into my fit of sobbing, and my throat seemed full of dry mud, and my chest rang like a hollow wall. I don't remember for how long I suffered before my sobbing rose once again into coughing and my coughing rose once again into laughter and my laughter changed into panting and then stopped. Then I had to close my jaws mainly by my will-power. Now they are closed. The rest of my body also is at rest. More or less. Except of course my heart and my brain. Which are throbbing like two immortal frogs. Every now and then some long-forgotten vein or rib also begins to vibrate. And some section of my gums begins to smart. And some fingertip begins to release a ray. And my head is pierced by an invisible nail or thorn. And I am reassured of the existence of my body. And of its capacity to foam and froth. But I have got to get out of this posture. But first I've got to describe it.

In the course of laughing and coughing and sobbing I must have rolled about in this hallway and crawled back into the room where, perhaps, I was before I came—I don't know how or why—to lie at the foot of the stairs. Which leads me to the conclusion that my body, nearly dead though it is, is still capable of miraculous movements. Which leads me inevitably to the conclusion that it is not as dead as I take it to be. I have overstated this last conclusion.

Anyway. I am in the living-room now. I am not sitting. Nor am I lying. Nor am I standing. Nor am I reclining. To tell the truth I have rarely been in this painful position before. No old sinner of my age can possibly attain it by his own effort or aspiration. My head is on the floor and my feet almost in the air. In other words my legs are open like a pair of scissors. My right leg seems suspended without any support. Like a wooden leg. No leg, wooden or not, can stand in air without any support. Mine, too, wouldn't have without the support of my right hand. But since I am writing this with my right hand, it couldn't be supporting my right leg, which leads me to a second guess that it is supported by that chair. The chair is green. My left leg is supported by my left hand. And perhaps by God. Because my left hand is virtually lifeless. This notebook is leaning against my right leg. I am writing in it, sitting on my neck. The tails of my shirt are touching my chin.

Between my legs hangs my poor penis. By its balls. Whenever my eyes meet its eye, I stop writing and begin to feel sorry for its forlorn state. Since it is not engaged in writing, it keeps staring at me and, perhaps, feels sorry for my forlorn state. I can't be sure, though, of its real feelings now. There was a time when I used to be. The fact that I am writing despite this difficult, though not impossible, posture, should give me an idea of my indestructible will and compulsiveness. This posture is, in fact, more suitable to the present inertness of my body. My only regret is that I haven't acquired it by my own effort, that I owe it to an accident, as explained above. I have to get out of it now, because suddenly my soles have begun to itch. I can't rub them against each other because they are facing the ceiling. And also because I can't twist or move them at will. Had there been a breeze, I would have requested it to caress them. If my legs were thrice as long, I could have used the ceiling for the necessary friction. It is at times like this that my companionlessness bothers me. And I miss the old woman. But she would have been in her own house even if she were alive. Perhaps by thinking of her I might have been able to move the itch to some other more private part. In my ideal society, every old person of my age will be provided with a nurse, male for a female, female for a male, and male for a male, female for a female in exceptional cases.

The point may be raised: From this particular point of view, those moribund societies are ideal where every young person is saddled with his old parents, or grandparents, or parents-in-law or grandparents-in-law, or in some cases by uncles and aunts of various kinds. I get the point, but, in my ideal society, family relationships will not determine the saddling, because there will be no family. To tell the truth, I am not sure or even clear about the details of my ideal society. But of this I am sure, that every young person will be required by law to serve at least one old person, sufficiently far gone, in every possible and impossible way. Of course, I will have discarded my body by then.

Krishna Baldev Vaid

The question may be raised: How is it that your tone has changed all of a sudden, that so soon after the dim reference to your ideal society you have begun to look like a withered owl? My answer would be: I've been suddenly assailed by the inevitability of my end and feel like crying myself to a sobful sleep, and I know I can't cry now. All I can do now is make a wry face. Which is what I am doing.

Seven

I've just finished eating something. I won't say what. I don't want to go into the details of my food. I never have. Those who forget in the evening what they ate in the morning are superior beings in my view. Those who cannot refrain from describing the meals of their characters are inferior writers in my view. Even the most beautiful woman looks no better than a sow when she is masticating her food. During the phase when I still had to keep in touch with the outside world, I never could bring myself to looking at a munching mouth. This often put me in peculiar quandaries. Not that I don't enjoy eating. I just don't want anyone else to see me doing it. Nor do I want to see anyone else doing it. Those who gloat over their meals and talk about their tastes are insufferable to me. During the phase when I was still invited out, I invariably threw up soon after returning home. I consider drinking less ludicrous than eating. Which doesn't mean I like descriptions of drinking. During the phase when I was still fond of books and movies, I often felt like tearing the pages and spitting at the scenes devoted to drinking and eating. In all of the numerous notebooks scattered all over this house, there is not a single description of eating and drinking. After I am gone, some people are bound to wonder what I ate and drank, whether I ate or drank at all.

The question may be raised—even if it has been before: Why do you keep filling these notebooks? My answer would be—even if it has been given before: What should I do instead; what can I? This answer is rude and unsatisfactory. Also ambiguous. Also dishonest. An answer should be so decisive that one doesn't have to add to or take anything from it. Such answers are not easily available. One can try all the same. One will. But before trying, I want to crack my knuckles for a while, at the risk of breaking my fingers. Risk and desire are inseparable friends.

My knuckles didn't crack crisply enough. Which is why I didn't enjoy cracking them. They sound like damp squibs.
    So the question was being raised, about my reasons for filling these notebooks. Let me attempt a detailed answer.

One reason is that it helps me to pass the time. Just as some other equally absurd occupations do. Apart from the time it takes to write a sentence, there is the enormous time it takes to wait for it before it is ready to be written. And the equally enormous time it takes to dread each word while it is being written. I can, if I like, call this whole process my dedication to the word, my selfless service. My own version of the notorious rock. Or my version of the raid on the inarticulate. I can degrade my absurdity with obvious allusions. My major reason, however, remains that it helps me to pass the time. Or to kill it. I know that time is neither passed nor killed. I know this method of passing or killing it is not original. But ever since I severed my connections with the outside world and let myself loose in this house, I have been won over, more completely than ever, to this method. Before that I was often lured by other methods, some of which seemed more enjoyable and less arduous. Of course, even then, I had a half-baked fixation for writing, but the fear of not being able to was strong enough to kill the desire.

Dying Alone

After I took refuge in this house, I realized that the only purpose of my life was to pass or kill time. By whatever means or madness I could. So I started filling these notebooks.

The question may be raised: Why were you afraid of not being able to write then, and why are you not afraid now? My answer would be: Because I was afraid I'd be read and criticized by others, also that I wouldn't be; in other words, at that time I didn't regard writing only as a way of passing or killing the time; at that time I wanted my writing to remain engraved forever on others' minds and hearts; which is why the work I did then differs from the work I do now, like sunshine from shade; I use 'work' only for convenience; in truth the word is inapplicable to what I did then, just as it is to what I do now, but since I have stopped fearing criticism, without stopping to crave praise, I write without constraint now. No, this is not true. If I were writing without constraint, I would have brought this house down by now. By the very mass of my misery.

Anyway. But for this addiction I wouldn't have been able to continue to crumble and endure my death, in this monstrous house, in this alien wasteland. I am caressing my own back now. I should feel embarrassed. I am beginning to be. There is no one to witness it. Except of course that devil. Who, for all I can see, is still around. Invisibly or otherwise. But he doesn't count. Even so, the very thought of his presence is enough to extinguish me. In a split second. At least for a while. For nothing but nothing can extinguish me permanently. I am inflating myself with the delusion that my irony is intact, more or less, even at this extremity. What irony! What extremity!

According to him irony also is illusory, this extremity also is unauthentic. He holds that any old man of my age and aspirations should be able to spend his last phase in absolute isolation, without any inhibition or anxiety, without any crutch or craving. Hence his obsessive suggestion that I should leave this house and follow him to the edge of that deserted road. And stand on its edge, hunchbacked. And moan ceaselessly. In order to transcend my pain. And my craving for panacea. When I see through his eyes, I see my irony and isolation riddled with flaws, my aspirations ordinary, my isolation incomplete, my dream of liberation no more than the nightmare of a would-be saint.

I must shake him off my mind. Before he materializes. The fear of my final confrontation with him is ever present in my mind, in my body, in my path. Like a chasm. Which will swallow me the moment I am off my guard.

Let me return to yet another aspect of my addiction to these notebooks. I am an irredeemable wordmonger. Which is another indication of my basic ordinariness. Paradoxically, also, my only medium of rising above it. Just as some people are fond of their private parts, which they take to be marvellous, or of caressing their private experiences, which they take to be singular, I am fond of fondling my private words. Which I take to be neither marvellous nor singular. That devil seems intent on depriving me of this secret vice. He says: No more of it now! He suggests: You have to go beyond this baseness. He says: You'll have to renounce your notebooks and your house and follow me. He says: Before you leave this world of ordinary tears, you have to devote yourself to yet another task, to yet another tune. Let him.

I want to admit without any reservation that I want them to be discovered. I want my notebooks to outlive me. I want them to be deciphered with the help of a pair of scholars from my own country. A Pundit and a Mullah. To be flown from over there. I want them both to condemn me and my work with one voice. And declare that the deceased was out of his mind. Or perhaps without one. That his literary remains are without any merit or method. That he only sought to seduce us with words. That these notebooks should be burnt or buried. Without any ceremony. I want this joint verdict to give rise to a rash of rumours in the literary circles all over the world, that an unknown exile has bequeathed tons of his droppings and scores of his notebooks to whosoever will accept them. That his mortal and literary remains contain the raw materials of numerous novels and plays, along with invaluable recipes for enduring time and eternity, particularly useful for the millions of ordinary old men all over the world. I want these rumours to result in wild appeals from all over the world for the preservation of my remains. I want these appeals to be kept up until the government and the National Literary Academy of my native country are irresistibly tempted to demand that my remains be repatriated or else they would consider cancelling diplomatic relations with the country of my exile. And then, in the midst of this clamorous controversy, my long-lost son should leap out of nowhere and assert his claim over the entire rubbish. By then everybody else should have become sick of the whole fuss. And that Pundit and Mullah should have fallen out with each other and returned to my native country. And then the natives of this town should turn to my long-lost son and offer the rubbish to him on the condition that he would let them have this house demolished so that a swimming pool can be built on this historic site, for the exclusive recreation of the old people of this God-forsaken town. And then my son should pocket the compensation and have my droppings and notebooks packed in proper gunny bags, and shipped to my native country. Where the government and the National Literary Academy should by then have turned against me. After realizing that they had been had by a madman. But my dutiful son should stubbornly hold them to their word and finally be rewarded by the discovery that my droppings can be made into a wonder drug. A panacea for all spiritual pains. Which should eventually earn him unearned millions. Which he should use for an endless supply of blank notebooks to gifted old people like myself all over the world. And he should continue to guard my notebooks with relentless zeal. Until he is able to discover a suitable scholar, willing to devote the rest of his days to them. And then that scholar should, at some advanced stage of his scrutiny, give it all up. And imprison himself in a monstrous house like this one. And spend the rest of his life in filling his own notebooks with ideas he has gleaned from mine. And he too should have an old woman living next door to him. And after she is gone, he too should imagine that one of his new neighbours, a nun, will one day appear at his doorstep. And he too should, in due course, accumulate tons of droppings and scores of notebooks. And after his death, the discovery of his remains, literary and mortal, should arouse a similar rumour in literary circles all over the world until. . . .

The question may be raised: Do you really desire all this or do you only imagine that you desire all this? My answer would be: I can't really say for sure, but I can say for sure that, if you were able to peep into the mind of an old exile, you would see desires more bizarre than this.

The question may be raised: Do you really think it is necessary for every old exile to keep a record of his wrath and writhing? My answer would be: Nothing, perhaps, is really necessary but, after a certain limit is reached or crossed, it helps to pretend that one's addictions are necessary; of course, there are those who have no addictions; but then those are the ones who cling to their progeny, or to their professions, or to others of their own age and inclinations, or to their memories, or to the benches in public parks, or to a Home, or to any other asylum, or to their unmade beds; of course, an unmade bed is fine as long as it is not surrounded by others—and one has taken to it not because of any ailment but only as an act of ineffectual defiance.

The question may be raised: Despite your exile, and your confinement, and your notebooks, and your rosaries, and your desire to rot without desire, you haven't attained total non-attachment, or else you wouldn't have fallen for the old woman, nor pinned your undying desire on your next-door neighbours, whom you mistake for anchoresses on no evidence other than your perverse intuition. I feel like sustaining this objection even though I can refute it by asserting, falsely, that my entanglement with the old woman was essentially desireless, that my desire for the non-existent anchoresses was essentially inflated. The anchoresses have brought the house next door to my mind again. It is quite likely it has been demolished. And a new mansion is fast taking its place. Or perhaps a swimming pool. To be reserved for the recreation of the senior citizenry. In which case I'll be able to drown in it some day. Death by drowning has always fascinated me. No, I am not totally unattached yet. If one of those anchoresses were to show up suddenly at my doorstep, I'm sure I'd be able to rise to my full height somehow. Or at least I'd be able to want to. In order to pierce her with my eyes. And my arrow. In an effort to forget that I am extinguished and she impenetrable. Despite my claim that my body is dead and my mind unattached. Despite also my preparedness to follow that devil to the edge of his deserted road. All of which prompts me to suggest that every old man who claims to have gone beyond desire should be continually tested. My guess is that he will fail every test. It is not for nothing that the inmates of old people's homes linger on and on. Their nurses keep them alive and lecherous. It is not for nothing that the patriarchs of extended families linger on and on. Their daughters-in-law keep them on their tottering toes.

The question may be raised: Are you pining for your extended family? My answer is: Obviously not, or else I wouldn't be dying by myself in this house, amidst my droppings, away from my kith and kin.

The question may be raised: Can you describe the state of your mind while you wrote the last sentence; in other words, can you tell whether you were grumbling or gloating or just indulging in yet another false sentiment? My answer is: You can deduce the state of my mind from that of my body, which was as follows: one of my hands was writing the sentence you picked on, the other picking my nose; one of my eyes was fixed on my notebook, the other on the grey hair my fingers had pulled out of my right nostril; after rubbing this hair into a tiny coil, I threw it away and started digging into my left nostril for another grey hair.

The question may be raised: Why are you still persisting in this dirty habit? My answer is: It helps me to write; besides, the slight pain I still experience, occasionally, while pulling out a hair, convinces me, against my better judgment, that I still am; even though, I should add, some of my nasal hairs come out so easily that one would think they are embedded in butter; needless to say, such hairs do not add much to my self-awareness, which is why, every now and then, I start pulling my nose instead, and wonder whether it is my nose or some other nuisance; it is at such moments that I feel the urge to see myself in a mirror, but there is no mirror around now, nor any other shining surface, for one day not too long ago, in a fit of jealousy, I broke all my mirrors and swallowed all the pieces.

I can't say why, but I feel like mentioning that I haven't shaved for ages; I haven't felt the urge to. In fact, I haven't done anything for ages, which could have gone without saying. In fact, nothing has been done to me for ages. Which is why my notebooks are cluttered with words like 'ages' and 'aeons' and 'centuries'. I've been inordinately aware of time and its tardiness. Which may explain my bondage to boredom. And my longing for eternity. Anyway. I had started to say something about my hair. My face has been hairless for ages. It feels like a soft-boiled but wrinkled egg. I like to imagine that all my hair disappeared one night when I was sourly asleep. The old woman used to complain that, in the dark, or without her magnifying glasses, she couldn't tell where my head ended and my face began. She couldn't tell whether she was licking

Dying Alone

my mouth or my nostrils, whether she was adoring my hands or my feet. She was one of those to whom all flesh feels the same. Her metaphysics often nauseated me. But this is not the time to start remembering her. I should concentrate on my hair, my nasal hair, by plucking which, even now, I occasionally get a faint awareness of myself. I sometimes wonder, though, whether it is hair or only my fine nasal dirt.

The question may be raised: But can't you get a faint awareness of yourself by plucking your pubic hair? My answer is: Alas! My private parts are absolutely bald now, like the rest of my body, including my chest, which was once so hairy; my chest, in fact, has changed into two sagging breasts, so much so that above my navel I am as good as an old woman. The old woman often wasted a lot of her energy in trying to arouse my breasts, or giving me some pleasure. I could never convince her that I had gone beyond the point of distinction between pain and pleasure. The old woman's own breasts were rather heavy and not quite as dead as mine; they never failed to rise a little to my desire.

The question may be raised: But can't you extract a faint awareness of yourself by plucking your breasts? My answer is: I wish I could. Let me add that quite often these days I can't find a single hair in either of my nostrils; then I panic and start twisting my nose, which feels like a cheap rubber toy.

The question may be raised: But why don't you play with your other toy? My answer is: Who says I don't, for I do, all the time, while writing as well as writhing. When I'm not playing with it, I'm staring at it as I sit on my haunches with my head hanging between my knees—like an old dog asking its older master: Which one of us is going to go first? I must add that I never get any answer from it as it continues to stare at the floor.

The question may be raised: But can't you get a faint awareness of yourself by shoving a finger or a fist up your arse? My answer is: This question can come only from a moron who doesn't know that after a stage even one's arse loses its sensitivity, and then neither a fist nor a burning rod can quicken it into any response; in fact, after a stage, even the haemorrhoidal arteries lose their life. Needless to boast, I have gone far beyond that stage.

I realize I have offered a self-portrait of sorts without really intending to. Now I am feeling embarrassed. The question may be raised: If you could remain silent about your food, why couldn't you about your body? My answer is: That is exactly what I am asking myself. But now that I have started, I can't stop. My face has often reduced me to wonder and amusement, but seldom to tears. It did so quite frequently when I was young. Aeons ago. Crying doesn't become an old man. Moaning is another matter, of course, because it is never without a modicum of measure. Laughing becomes an old man even less. Smirking is another matter, of course, for it is never without a modicum of suffering. Obviously, I haven't yet gone beyond the point of distinction between smirking and laughing, between crying and moaning, between music and noise. Those who have gone beyond that point can laugh, if they wish, like hyenas, because their laughter then is as good as howling.

The objection may be raised: How can you say anything credible about others, for haven't you been totally cut off from them, thanks to your confinement for the past century or so in this monstrous house? My answer is: I wish I had been totally cut off, for the truth is that, despite my confinement to myself in this monstrous house for the past century or so, I am still in touch with all the fundamental torments of everybody, which is one reason I am still so vulnerable to that devil who keeps luring me to the edge of that deserted road.

But let me return to my body. I have already described my bald head and alluded to my bald private parts. But I want to dwell on my head a little longer. It is hairless but, despite its apparent similarity to a soggy papaya, impregnable like a rock. This is due to years of head-beating. Before I took refuge in this monstrous house, whenever I was up against a wall or found dying difficult, I started beating my head vigorously instead of holding it in my hands like other sensible sufferers. Invariably, when I was alone; occasionally even when others were around. At that time this habit seemed like a sure symptom of insanity; now it seems all I was doing was beating my skull into immunity to all external assaults. As long as I had hair, I often felt, while running my hand over my head, that it was grass bursting out of concrete. Now my head is all concrete. If a blind person were to caress my body, from my hard head down to my soft root, he or she would take me for a clumsy puppet put together by a bad artist. If a person with vision were to . . . but why would a person with vision bother to caress my body?

The objection may be raised: But if it is a true picture of your head, why did you record earlier that your old woman couldn't tell where your head ended and your face began? My answer is: The old woman was a veritable idiot, blinded by passion, or at least so she seemed to me.

To continue: below the head there is my narrow forehead, a closed door, through which, infrequently, a half-baked idea, or a dim memory, or a rotten sentiment enters my miserable mind. Am I drawing an invidious distinction between my head and my forehead? Of course, I am. That is how I rule over my dead body—by drawing invidious distinctions—if, of course, I may be permitted to call my body 'body' and my nominal claim over it as my rule. Even if I am not permitted to do so, I will maintain that every limb of my body is either antagonistic or indifferent to every other limb. My head, especially, has lost all contact with the rest of me, especially with my forehead, whose skin hangs like a flimsy curtain over the closed door to which I referred a moment before.

My neck cannot boast of any special quality, but, whenever I encircle it with my hand, and close my eyes, I feel I am holding my wrinkled root, or some stolen chicken's neck, or the limp leg of a hare-like idea. In other words, it is still capable of producing a variety of wrong impressions. If I use my imagination perversely enough, I can still derive perverse pains by fondling it. As a matter of fact, if I use my imagination perversely enough, I can transform every limb of mine into every other limb and derive the appropriate pain from it. After a flood or a drought or an earthquake one ceases to be finicky and is grateful for any piece of muck in one's mouth. Similarly, at the extremity I have reached, I am able to use my belly as my feet, my feet as my hands, my hands as my legs, my mouth as every other part of my body except my knees, and derive the desired pain.

But why am I forgetting my face, which, after all, is the king of one's appearance? The face of every old person, after a certain stage, resembles that of an infant's, more or less sick, more or less ugly. My face is no different. Since I have no mirrors around now, I can't say for sure. But, whenever I run my hand over it, I am never sure whether I am touching my eyes or my nostrils, my lips or my gums, my chin or my cheeks. Occasionally, however, I feel I am caressing a couple of dead and dry frogs huddled together. It is futile, in other words, to describe a face that is so unreliable. The old woman used to condemn my mouth and ears most whenever she condemned my face. She often said that, if I had no ears, or had less of them, and if I didn't have a mouth that roamed all over my face, she wouldn't have wondered as much as she did at the capriciousness of my maker. I was never offended by her remarks because I could see she was ridiculing my maker as much as my face.

Dying Alone

I notice I have again fallen into the foul arms of my old woman. I want to close my eyes a while in order to release myself from her embrace. Perhaps, on opening them, I will find that I have released myself from the idiotic necessity of describing my face. Perhaps my eyes will never open again. I doubt if I'll be so lucky.

I want to start this sitting with a regret: I wish I had fathered a child. He would have been my brother by now. Perhaps I did father one and have forgotten all about him. But if I had he would have been sitting beside me. Bragging about his achievements. Or beating me. I would have poured my heart out to him. He would have shouted: Why can't you speak clearly? I would have closed my mouth and tried to communicate through sign language: My dear son, you have to bear with my inability to speak clearly. It is odd I should think of my unfathered child as a son. Or perhaps it isn't. I can't conceive of quarrelling with a daughter. Of course, there are those who don't think anything of quarrelling with their daughters, but I consider them beneath contempt. If I had a son, he would be glowering at me now. I would have glowered back. I would have let my mouth hang like a frog's; I would have thrashed the air with my hands; I would have tried to torment him with mute accusations; I would have let my head wobble; I would have pushed my dentures out with my tongue; I would have farted; I would have belched; I would have chewed the ends of my moustache; I would have smacked my lips; I would have wet my legs; I would have grumbled about my lack of appetite; in short, I would have done everything to make him feel guilty.

I don't know whether it is because of this regret or some other hidden horror but just now I've been seized by the desire to start moaning in a voice so loud and lacerating as to induce all other old people dying in their several houses along this street to join me in moaning in voices so loud and lacerating as to induce all the other old people dying in their several houses all over this country to join us in moaning in voices so loud and lacerating as to induce all the other old people dying in their several houses all over the world to join us in moaning in voices so loud and lacerating as to induce everybody all over the world to take our moaning for the moaning of the entire mankind so much so that all the saints and scientists should drop everything and start searching for an effective way of silencing us, and after they have failed they should all congregate outside this monster of my house while I watch them from my upstairs window, fingering one of my rosaries, smiling with unabashed arrogance, as I see them feeling intimidated by my half-naked half-dead body but overawed by the void oozing out of my eyes, and after tantalizing them with my deep silence for a long spell I should howl out of the reach of their comprehension, and that of my own, and they should be so bewitched by my performance, purged by now of all recognizable connection with the initial occasion, that they should forget what that occasion was and start howling in unison with me, doing their best to keep up with my pitch and purity, and then finally my next door neighbours, those non-existing nuns, should materialize and interrupt their prayers and other holy pursuits and come out of their closets and start gaping at me and discover in my half-naked half-dead alien body the figure of a refulgent Messiah, and then their eyes should sparkle with tears, even as I raise my hand and stop everybody's screams and say in a serene voice: Kneel so that I can arise! And then with one strong pull I should succeed in flying out of this net of illusions, this world of ordinary tears, and then everybody should see me suspended in midair, above their heads, and burst into a hymn, and then I should shout SILENCE, and they bow their heads and I fly out of their ken, and when they recover they should be so astonished as to forget why they had come there, and then, of course, they should return to their worldly woes, while away from them, in some other upper region, I should start another round of my quest for the peace and unity that eluded me down here, that will elude me up there.

The freak fantasy recorded above, was, perhaps, an outcome of my eagerness to end. I should, therefore, put together, before it is too late, a few dark suggestions which may or may not alleviate anyone's anxiety or boredom or incompleteness, which may not even enable them to endure their anxiety or boredom or incompleteness, but, which will, perhaps, enable them to entertain fond hopes of some relief in the indefinite future.

My first suggestion: Confront every WHY with WHY NOT violently enough to shatter both of them; but since such violence is given only to a chosen few, this suggestion is for the chosen few.

My second suggestion: Submit every deed, doubt, desire, regret, dread, surprise, quest, defeat, qualm, and so on, to WHY so that you can confront it with WHY NOT, even though it is given only to a chosen few to do so with a violence sufficient for shattering both WHY and WHY NOT. The point is that WHY and WHY NOT should be continually pitted against each other even if you lack the violence necessary for shattering both. The question may be raised: But is it necessary to do so? The answer is: It may or may not be necessary, but it will be beneficial.

My third suggestion: Try to believe that nothing is necessary; this will make everything not only easy but also impossible.

Which leads to my inevitable fourth suggestion: Only that which is impossible, or almost so, is easy; I am afraid it will be futile to try to unravel this paradox.

My fifth suggestion: As long as one is alive, one cannot rise above the basic animal needs—food, sex, pain and shelter; the extent and intensity of these needs can be reduced but never denied. The question may be raised: Isn't this suggestion soiled? The answer is: Which suggestion is not?

Krishna Baldev Vaid

My sixth suggestion: After entering the final phase of one's life, one should waste all one's time in unbroken solitude; three of the basic needs should then be taken care of by the state or society, the fourth, namely sex, by one's own inadequate imagination.

My seventh and last suggestion will be expressed not in sentences, or sentence fragments, but in a random selection of my favourite words. The question may be raised: But won't it remain an enigma to others? Three answers are: Yes, it will; it is not essential to understand the last suggestion; there is none other.

So then those words are: Sky. Sea. Mud. Silence. Sigh. Depth. Intensity. Horizon. Bog. Fire. Ashes. Dark. Time. Panacea. Tone. Prayer. Perhaps. Trance. If. Bird. Flower. Mind. No. Flesh. Shit. Root. Grave. Or. Word. Air. Death. But. Desire. Terror. And. Limit. Awareness. Horror. Dust. Point. Doubt. Night. Disgust. Longing. End. Greed. Shore. Bosom. Void. Red. Past. Breath. God. Empathy. Why. Why not.

Eight

I am upstairs now. I do not know how or when or why I came—or was brought—here. Nor do I want to.

I'd like to imagine that my own will worked this miracle.

I do not know what time it is. Nor do I want to.

I do not know where he is now. Nor do I want to.

I do not know what will become of me now. Nor do I want to.

I do not know for how many aeons more I have to endure this life, this death, this house, this phase. Nor do I want to.

I do not know whether my indifference indicates my release from this life, this death, this house, this phase, or whether it is a passing impatience. Nor do I want to.

I am in my moan-room, on my knees, behind a closed window that opens on the street, like a sinner about to pray. Underneath my knees are two cushions. In front of me is a low stool on which sits this notebook in which I am recording all this.

I am soaring in an unfamiliar sky now. Surrounded by silence. I cannot say in what way this silence is different from other silences. Nor do I want to.

I want to break off all my limbs, one by one, and cast them away, one by one, as I soar.

I see my limbs strewn on the street below and my eyes perched on a high mound, watching the pieces of my body lying around it.

I do not know why this sight has failed to disturb me. Nor do I want to.

Now I see him soaring along with me, his face glowing with victory, his eyes reflecting the edge of that deserted road where he wants me to stand, hunchbacked, and moan ceaselessly. I do not know why he wants me to. Nor do I want to.

I do not know whether that edge will mark the last point of my pain. This I want to know.

Dying Alone

I am afraid he has divined my desire and started soaring higher.

I know I must keep up with him. I do not know why. Nor do I want to.

Now we are soaring in one form.

I do not know whether we will stand on the edge of that deserted road, hunchbacked, in one form, and moan ceaselessly in one voice. Nor do I want to.

Short Stories

Silence

I can see the little waterfall from where we are sitting. The atmosphere is drenched with its melody. Sometimes it wafts so close to me that I feel I can catch and kiss it. But the breeze plays tricks on me, and I am left trembling with uncomfortable vibrations. I experience a similar sensation when I see a flash of lightning.

My eyes are fixed on the waterfall. It seems I am watching an opportunity slipping by. I close my eyes. Now I feel it is raining somewhere, far away, or perhaps it is someone calling someone —me—from some other shore, tenderly, again and again.

When we sat down I thought we were going to have a heart-to-heart talk; I was so full. I am, even now. I have always wanted to thaw the silence of years between me and my friend. Every effort has been followed by a fresh layer.

But just now this silence appears to be quite natural. Words are futile; silence is the essence. Or so it seems at the moment. The thought of either of us breaking it appals me; it will be no less than a violation of something ineffable. No, words are quite futile. . . .

The silence, the solitude, the house and the lullabies of the little waterfall. . . . A seductive atmosphere whose tones are so dim, so elusive.

My friend is also gazing at the waterfall. His face is blank. My stare doesn't disturb the smooth surface of his absence. It would appear that we are waiting for a third person to come and link us together. It is a foolish thought. I want to convey it to him. I can't prod him with my looks. And a word, I feel, will be an insult to the atmosphere. I turn my eyes away to the house.

The house is very old. Years ago it was built by a prince from Hyderabad. He used to spend a couple of months here every year. He had built the house, in fact, for his favourite queen. The queen died during one of their sojourns. The prince developed a distaste for the place; it remained unoccupied for years. After the prince's death one of his sons sold it to my friend. No one wanted to buy the deserted house and the son needed money. Just about that time my friend had married Amina and decided to live away from the city.

My friend has made a minimum of alterations in the house. From a distance, even now, it looks quite deserted. At dusk a deep sadness descends on it; one can't sit indoors. Some people believe it is haunted. Amina laughs at the idea. My friend doesn't. But he has never expressed his opinion overtly. Sometimes he gives me the impression of just tolerating Amina. I prefer this way of dealing with mutual differences; it means so much less argument.

I don't know what Amina thinks of it, though. I tried to sound her out in the beginning. I can't say I got much out of the attempt. During those days I used to imagine all sorts of things—that Amina must be finding my friend's elderly air of understanding rather oppressive, that she would prefer an occasional argument, that she would like to live in a big city. It was, I guess, all wishful thinking. I feel a lot better about their relationship now.

I feel I am shrinking under this introspection. I look at him. Why is he so blank? He hasn't spoken a word to me throughout the day. And yet he wrote me five letters urging me to come over. He should have said something. But then he is strange.

In one of the rooms there is a portrait of the deceased queen. It is a dim old portrait, and I don't consider it striking or unusual in any way. A woman of normal charms, lost in thought, looking dreamily at something. But my friend often contemplates it with great absorption. Once, I remember, Amina remarked jocularly: I wish this picture were not there; it frightens me so!

I tried to detect some serious criticism of my friend implicit in the joke. I took it to be a disapproval of my friend's pose. Perhaps I wanted the joke to have this implication. I recall how in those days I used to be always sulking. Now it is clear that all those flaws in their marriage were imaginary.

They have been married three years.

I don't know how long my own marriage will absorb me to the exclusion of everything else; I am looking forward to that absorption.

My friend has a way of keeping himself aloof from everything, every experience. He never lets himself go, is always self-locked. He strikes some people as a mere poseur. But I know he is helpless. I had fears that he would be misunderstood by Amina; the fears were more like hopes. I am happy that that stage is over. He loves Amina. I believe marriage has done more for him than he knows.

I am thrilled once again at the idea of breaking the silence of years. I want to tell him about Salima. I want to, well, just talk about any trivial thing. I wish I could tell him just how happy I am at this moment. I want to say something silly so that both of us can burst into laughter. I have a vague idea of what I should say. But I can't find the proper words, nor enough courage. I fear I will never reach the end of my sentence. He will quietly hear me to the extent I go; the rest of it will remain unexpressed; it will keep festering inside. No, I won't make the attempt.

Besides the portrait of the queen my friend had found a little casket lying in a corner. It contained scores of letters to the queen from a friend of her husband's. These letters were my friend's chief preoccupation for several days. Amina was never told anything about them. He even forbade me to do so. I think I would have told her otherwise. I get a perverse satisfaction from relating stories of infidelity to women; it gives me the feeling of having established something. Amina could not have noticed the casket. Or perhaps he put her off with a lie. He tells lies quite casually for reasons that are not always obvious. Had she asked me directly I think I would have told her all I knew in spite of his instructions.

He wanted to write a novel about the queen. The idea didn't appeal to me much. Perhaps he wants to read the novel or its first draft to me. He should have mentioned it in his letters. He has said nothing about it anyway since my arrival.

I don't really regret the trip. Even without his letters I would have come. I have been away from him for too long a period this time. I expected him to ask me why.

Had Amina been here I would have told everything unasked. I can talk quite freely to him when someone else is present. It was so even in our college days.

I don't understand why our reserve has increased with intimacy. Sometimes I have doubts about this intimacy itself.

The house is surrounded by a garden. It is not quite a garden. There are a few flowers but no flowerbeds. There is grass but it is never mown. The gardener who used to look after it for the prince now does the cooking. There are a few fruit trees but they don't bear fruit. There is a pair of dead trees; they look like two coarse-skinned arms lifted upwards. I have often tried to guess their ages. Most of the other trees are very tall; they come to life morning and evening, with birds. After sunset these whispers that I hear now will rise to a pitch that will make it difficult for me to keep the music of the waterfall separate from them. This mixture always bothers me; it will bother me today.

At noon, if the sun is bright, the place looks desolate enough for a recluse. The silence of the night produces a different effect, that of horror. Even the waterfall sings a frightened note.

Amina often takes a stroll in the garden all by herself, giving a peculiar little jerk to her head. Once I made a remark about this. She smiled. I felt she was evading the remark. My friend was also with us at that time. I remember having thought that but for his presence she would have added a few words to her smile. When we are all together she doesn't talk much. Had she been here now she would have been walking about at a distance from us. I would have been looking at her, thinking perhaps of the reasons of what

Silence

I would have regarded as her restlessness. Every time I see her strolling in the garden I think she looks like a shadow.

There are very few things in the house and those that are there do not suggest the presence or the status of Amina. A few pictures, most of them old; a few sculptures, most of them stone. The doors are always open and there are no curtains. In the porch there are four wicker chairs around a rectangular table with stone legs. Four cactus plants occupy the four corners of the table. I have a private myth about these cactuses; I imagine Amina some night charmed four of their guests into this shape. There is no stain of domesticity in the house. Sometimes Amina strews a few flowers and leaves before the sculptures and burns incense, and the house assumes the atmosphere of a cave temple.

Last evening when I arrived here I saw a heap of yellow leaves in the porch. They produced an eerie noise under our feet. Even otherwise I noticed some symptoms of waste. I looked towards my friend for an explanation; he looked away. I wanted to gather up all those leaves and throw them out. I didn't though.

The living-room is generally full of Amina's books lying about in natural disorder. Some of her clothes are also often seen heaped up in a cradle. I saw neither books nor clothes last evening. I have never been able to account for this cradle. Every time it looks newer than before. I have always wanted to make a joke about this with Amina.

He was looking at the portrait of the queen. But this used to be in the porch on the wall opposite the table? I was on the verge of a significant query when the gardener-cook came in. Now I have only a vague memory of the significance; I've forgotten the exact enquiry. I guess I don't have a good memory.

Had I known Amina wouldn't be here, I would have delayed my visit in spite of his letters.

I will go back tomorrow. But for his curious insistence I would have come only after the big event. It would have been a big surprise for both of them. I will leave tomorrow morning by the first train.

I am afraid we are not going to have even the briefest of conversation, unless it happens at dinner tonight. He is still gazing at the waterfall.

The chirping of the birds sprinkles over the music of the waterfall. It is getting darker every moment. Amina would have turned the lights on by now. There are several lamps but all of them are covered by shades that stifle rather than cover the light. Once Amina expressed a desire to remove all these lampshades. She said she wanted naked light. But my friend looked at her so pathetically that she laughed and said: I won't touch them; don't look a martyr, please. I remarked that at least one of the bulbs should be naked. He kept quiet. Amina reduced her laughter to a neutral smile. I felt positively bitter that day about the fact that they were married. I had a perverse desire to watch an angry exchange between them.

Not that Amina has never disagreed with him. But she is always rather cautious. I told her once that she should not be afraid of hurting him for he had in him the hardness of stone. I don't know why I said it and on what precise occasion. She just smiled as if she knew better. That exactly is the trouble with her. She meets whatever you say with a smile that is open to several interpretations. I used to spend considerable time figuring some of these interpretations out.

Sometimes we get involved in some stupid argument over some problem of a bookish nature. Amina at once assumes the role of an uninterested listener. She never participates in the discussion, but her presence is a promise that somebody is perhaps after all weighing all we say with more or less impartiality. I always am the first to give in. I feel she doesn't like arguments to crystallize into serious disagreements.

Soon it will be completely dark. Darkness and silence combined overwhelm me completely. I hope it won't get any darker tonight. The moon is there.

For a moment we happen to look straight at each other. I smile; he looks away. I want to get up and yell at him. But my desires are always too easily suppressed.

Last evening he was at the railway station to receive me. He was alone. I thought Amina might be ill. On the way home I asked him what he was doing. He said, 'Nothing.' He put me the same question. I shrugged my shoulders. It seemed we had expressed our occupations through symbols.

I was thinking of his letters. Each of the five letters had read like a telegram: Come if you can for a couple of days.

When we were young we used to write long letters to each other often, even when we were in the same town. Each new experience, place or acquaintance provided a subject for analysis and description. Sometimes we put in verses from some favourite poet, French or English. I have a bundle of those letters. During the last so many years I have received only one long letter from him. That was just a few days after his marriage. On reading that I felt he was relaxing after a long pilgrimage, retrospecting about its difficulties, feeling a little satisfied and a little overwhelmed that it had ended.

On reaching the house, when I didn't see Amina, I thought he had called me just because of that. With Amina away he must have felt too lonely to enjoy the solitude of the place. He could have come down to Bombay, but he hates the place. So do I.

I hope now I shall be able to spend a couple of months in this house every year. Salima approves of the idea. There is a little cottage attached to the house. I think it is vacant. I must not forget to ask him to have it fixed up. He may ask me why, I will have to tell him in that case. No, I won't tell him anything. I have a superstition that if I tell people about my plans they never come to anything.

Last night it felt so strange to be eating alone with him. Amina's chair was empty. I kept looking at it. Had she been there I wouldn't have looked that way so much. He sits next to her; while eating he keeps looking at that picture just as some people keep looking at their hands while talking. Last evening, however, he didn't raise his head from his plate even once.

I wanted to ask him about Amina. After dinner you cannot talk here. The day comes to an abrupt end with that. Even whispers produce long queer echoes. Every word you utter keeps haunting the house for long after. Besides, one has a fear of being overheard by someone in the dark.

Before I could make up my mind he got up and went to his room. I sat, my head bent and my hands interlocked behind it. I could have been praying. Finally I got up, gathered the leaves before the sculptures and threw them out. An offering to darkness!

Since this morning he hasn't spoken a word to me. It irritates me a little. But isn't my irritation absurd?

Once he remarked that his loneliness had not gone in spite of marriage and Amina. He said it in a tone that suggested some kind of triumph. I had thought he had married only in order to fill the vacuum. But I had my doubts. When I saw Amina all my doubts turned into plain envy; it is no use denying that now.

It is quite possible he had talked of the persistence of his essential loneliness in order to console me. This was just after their marriage. During that visit, he said and did several things out of an exasperating solicitude for me.

I have thought of marriage so many times during the past three years. But the demands of one's age are different, also its limitations. The number and intensity of enthusiasms have gone down and the fear of risks has increased. One can't take a leap into the dark. It is difficult to close one's eyes; one is not dazzled enough by anything.

But my friend must have been dazzled enough by Amina. I have never been able to know the story of their coming together. I didn't ask and he never told me.

Their example, however, must have inspired me. If I could find someone like Amina, someone beyond the categories of the beautiful and the unbeautiful, someone who would take everything with a smile, someone who would fit in anywhere in any situation, someone a little sad, something of a woman, something of a girl. . . .

But all this looked impossible. It is very rare for two persons to have an absolutely similar set of opportunities. It is absurd to follow anybody in the hope that you would arrive at the same place. This thought sobered me. I started giving concessions to every woman. Things came to such a pass that I was prepared to accept any one. It is sheer luck that I am going to escape the consequences of this desperation. The combined weakness of head and heart could have plunged me into any abyss.

Salima was reassurance incarnate at the very first sight. She survived even my subsequent discriminations. She seemed to have left the buoyancy of youth behind, but had retained some of its more enduring charms. The flames had given place to a warm, stable fire. After a couple of meetings we attained a level of intimacy that would have been impossible in youth. It is not quite correct that one is rash in youth. One has too much time then. One can afford to progress leisurely from one level to another.

I was with Salima the evening before last. We went to the beach. The sea looked so small that I kept thinking of this waterfall.

I told her about Amina and my friend, I think for the first time. She was perhaps thinking of something; she gave a start. I told her she resembled Amina in so many ways. Then I closed my eyes to see those ways. I couldn't locate any particular resemblance. It was then that I told her that after marriage we should spend some time here. While listening to the story about the house she became a little sad. That pleased me, her sadness.

Perhaps the greatest resemblance between Amina and Salima is this touch of sadness. I don't know.

I like sad women anyway. Amina carries about her a flavour of unhappiness which seems to be the essence of the pain of living.

At the mention of the waterfall Salima smiled a little. The smile illumined her sadness and her resemblance with Amina further. She asked me where the water came from, how much was the height, whether the sound increased at night, whether I sometimes mistook the waterfall for the sea with a chastened noise, particularly at night. . . . She began to pant with the rush of questions. Then she said she wanted to dream about the waterfall at night. I felt happy to think that she had asked so many questions about the waterfall and so few about my friend and Amina.

Before leaving her at her house I quietly mentioned my intention to visit my friend. In fact, I almost asked her permission, explaining that I had received five insistent letters. She replied that there was no hurry about the ceremonies and that we could talk about the final arrangements on my return. She didn't even ask me for how many days I would be away. I was happy. I always feel a little scared at the inevitable restrictions of married life; you have to explain so much, tell so much, conceal so much.

I'll tell her much more about this place when I go back. Perhaps I will tell her about Amina's absence and my friend's silence. And also about the cactuses about which I don't remember having told her that evening.

Very soon the trees, the grass, in fact the entire darkness will start throbbing with fireflies. The last chirpings of the birds raise bubbles in the dark silence. The bubbles will subside. The moon is threatened by two patches of clouds.

I can't even see him clearly now. He has started smoking. The dark hills beyond the waterfall have slipped very close to us. It looks like we are being besieged on all sides. One patch of cloud has given itself to the moon.

Amina also smokes. Whenever I see a cigarette between her lips I feel a curious sensation in my body. I have a strong impulse to snatch the cigarette, and to kill her. Once I told her about this in a casual way. She lit another cigarette. I was at once tense. She threw the cigarette away. I had been caught red-handed, as it were.

I told Salima how a beautiful woman smoking drives me wild. She said she would start smoking after marriage, and she laughed.

Amina laughs rarely. But when she does you can see soft carpets being unrolled before you.

The house is still unlit. The chairs stand out in the dark. I can't see the cactuses. He is lighting another cigarette. I want to peer behind his face in the glow of the cigarette. The gardener's cottage is also dark. The moon is completely vanquished. The bubbles have subsided.

—Won't you say something?
—Let's go in.

He gets up and looks at me without allowing me time to look back at him.

—Aren't you hungry?

Silence

His sentence falls like a corpse before me.
—When is Amina coming back?

He starts walking towards the house. I follow him as if in pursuit of an answer to my question. I am not sure if he has heard it at all; it was barely audible.

The moon is buried under the clouds.

As we approach the steps leading to the porch, he turns round.
—I am going back tomorrow. I feel surprised at the tone of my voice.
—Well!
—I'll be back very soon.
—Amina won't be here even then.

So he did hear my question. I try to pause, but can't.

—When is she coming back?
—She is not coming back.
—I don't understand you.
—I didn't understand her either when she told me so.

The gardener has turned the lights on. He is setting the table now. The moon is alive once again. We are mounting the steps. Our shadows are with us.

I don't know what has happened between my friend and Amina. I am sure I am not going back tomorrow. I don't think I will be able to explain myself to Salima but I am sure I am not marrying her. I'll drop her a line. Will she understand? I don't care.

The Stone of a Jamun

The bus-stop was deserted. The row of government quarters on the other side of the road had gone to sleep under the lashes of the sun. The makeshift shelter above my head seemed angry, perhaps because I was the only passenger there. I looked at my watch. I was afraid it would stop any second because of my anxiety about the new tuition I was going to start that day. I wound it up again and realized I was ruining its springs with my frequent overwindings.

A bead of sweat rolled slowly to the tip of my long nose, hesitated, and plunged. It was soon followed by another, which was soon followed by still another, which ... I tried to make a game out of making them fall roughly at the same spot but then I got bored and breathless. I started wiping my face and forehead with my nose-rag. It was soon soaking wet. My lips had dried long ago. Had my rag been a little less filthy, I might have squeezed it into my mouth.

I was standing under the shelter but couldn't shake off the impression that it was standing under me. I was very lonely. I wanted a companion in my misery so that I could tell him we were having the hottest spell of summer, or that the public transport system in Bombay and Calcutta was far superior to ours, or some

The Stone of a Jamun

other piece of irrefutable nonsense.

I already had several coats of stench and sweat all over my face, forehead, neck and forearms, and a part of my chest; and cursed the girl I was going to coach; and damned myself; and rued the day I decided to earn my living as a private tutor. But all that, I knew, wouldn't quicken our tardy transport system, nor would it improve the awful condition of our country. And I was worried I'd be late. And I was mortally afraid of losing the job and of being rebuked by that girl's ugly mother.

But the fact remained that, in my anxiety and eagerness, I had reached the bus-stop a couple of hours too early. I'd just started reproaching myself for this when I was interrupted by the question that everybody keeps asking everybody else in our country—What time is it, Mister?

I turned my head and barked—One-twenty-five!

—I don't think that bugger from the municipal committee will bother me now, he muttered, obviously for his own comfort, and walked off to the shacks behind the bus-stop. I felt like overtaking him and shouting: I am that bugger from the municipal committee! Of course, I didn't do that.

After some time I saw him returning to the bus-stop, with a primitive weighing balance suspended from his hand, looking like a homespun image of justice. A boy followed him, at a distance of a few steps, carrying a huge basket heaped with jamuns on his little head. I felt grateful now for the company.

—It's so hot today, I said to him

He paid me no attention.

—Fetch the other basket also, he ordered the boy.

The boy dashed off to those shacks. The man was trying to balance the basket on the uneven ground and muttering curses at the bugger from the municipal committee. Presently the boy came back with the other basket, which looked a little bigger than the first. He was accompanied now by another boy who was obviously his younger brother. The man was still busy trying to balance the other basket, so the boy had to wait with that weight on his head. His brother looked at the jamuns in the other basket and said—You promised you'd share, remember!

The boy stood straining under the huge basket, his arms stretched like rubber bands and his skin like leather. The man finally helped him take the load off his head and said—Well done, you son of a lion! Now for the other two, run!

The boy ran off. His brother followed for a few steps but then decided to return to the jamun-seller. He had no rags on. The man held the basket with both his hands and looked around desperately for a brick or something to prop it with. I stepped forward and said—Let me hold the basket while you go look for a brick or something. He scanned me and decided I didn't look reliable enough.

—The boy will be back soon; I'm in no hurry.

The boy came back with the third basket, which looked even bigger than the first two, but then I was already prejudiced against the man. This time the boy managed to take the basket off his head and put it on the ground, all by himself, without spilling a single jamun. No, he had spilled one. His brother made a dash for it but the boy was quicker. He wiped the jamun on his palm and placed it on the basket. The man had seen everything.

—Now get me two bricks from over there!

The man's order sounded like a punishment for the work that boy had done so far. The boy ran off, picked two bricks, started running back to the jamun-seller, dropped one brick on his foot, retrieved it, and limped toward the baskets.

Meanwhile I had dried my nose-rag by waving it about in the sun.

The boy's foot was bleeding. His brother pointed to it and shouted—Blood! The boy took a pinch of dust and sprinkled it over his bleeding toes

—Shall I go for the fourth one now?

His tone, however, suggested that they ought to sell the three he'd already fetched and leave the fourth in reserve.

—What are you waiting for? Run!

The boy ran off. This last basket didn't seem very heavy, for the boy came back running, but then it could be that he was doing this to impress his master, if not me. His brother met him halfway this time, and they had a brief conference, after which the boy transferred the basket onto his brother's head, held it with one hand, and led him back to the jamun-seller.

—I carried this one, said the little boy.

—More bricks?

—What? Oh yes, of course, more bricks. We can always use more bricks.

The jamun-seller spoke as if he was granting a favour reluctantly. The boy ran off for the bricks. He'd overcome the injury to his foot. His brother stood near the jamun-seller as he spread the juiciest of the jamuns on the top of one of the baskets as so many baits for his customers.

—Here are the bricks!

He carried four this time on his shoulder.

—Put them down.

The boy put them down one by one.

—Get four more so that I can make a seat for myself.

The boy ran off.

—Shall I go too? his brother asked the jamun-seller.

—You! The man laughed.

I joined him with a sheepish smile as he looked at me. My nose-rag had become wet again. I wanted to ask that man about my bus. He would know. But will he answer me? The arrogant wretch! The boy was faster than my bus. More reliable too! He was already back, this time with six bricks. After he'd put them down, I noticed a few bruises on his bare shoulders. The orange brick powder was all over his belly and back.

—You want me to make a seat for you?

—Yes.

—You want me to sweep the ground first?

—There's no need for that.

But the boy was perhaps meticulous by nature. He squatted down and started sweeping the ground with his hands; his brother too sat down, peeled his eyes off the jamuns, and started sweeping the ground. A splinter pierced the boy's palm, and he concentrated on catching it between his nails and pulling it out. He looked very intelligent as he did that.

—Isn't he a smart boy? The man smiled at me as he said that.

—He certainly is. Your son, I take it?

The man laughed in a way I didn't like at all.—Come on, Mister! Don't you see the colour of his skin?

I paid him no attention. The boy had prepared a nice seat for him. The jamun-seller took off his shoes and shirt and sat down on his throne. He looked very smug. Perhaps he'll take off his dhoti soon enough and start shouting at every passer-by—Buy my jamuns or else I'll wave this at you!

—Shall I go for the box of weights now?

—Oh yes! Do you know where it is? No, you better stay here and watch the baskets; I'll go for the weights myself; there's some change in that box.

He winked at me in a way I didn't like at all.

—I too will watch the baskets, the boy's brother said.

The jamun-seller paid him no attention and said to me—You keep an eye on them, mister; after all, they're kids. I didn't like the way he appointed me as their guard.

He looked back at us from a distance to assure himself that we hadn't all gone wild and irresponsible. After he disappeared round the corner, the little boy asked his big brother—Can I take one, just one? The boy looked at me and said—No.

I kept quiet.

—I am going to take one, just one.

He reached for the basket. I kept quiet. The boy looked at me. His brother looked at him.

—Just one!

—No, the boy said.

Had they referred their dilemma directly to me, I too would have said no. The boy and I exchanged a smile. His brother withdrew his hand and started to sulk.

The jamun-seller had perhaps started an argument with his wife or something, for he was taking longer than the boy had taken on his trips. The little boy was edging closer to the baskets. He was almost sniffing them now. He would have picked up a couple of jamuns with his lips, had the boy not admonished him in time—Will you get back!

I decided to make small talk with the elder boy.

The Stone of a Jamun

—Does the jamun-seller live in one of those shacks?
—Yes.
—You work for him?
—Yes.
—Is he related to you then?
— No. He is our bread-giver!
I liked his mischievous smile.—And your parents?
—They're dead.
I decided to change the subject.—When is the next bus coming?
—Who knows! Buses don't run on time.
I smiled at his knowing tone.
—Put it down! Or else I'll tell him! the big boy shouted.
The little boy had taken advantage of our conversation, and had pilfered a jamun which was very close to his open mouth now.
—Put it down! Or else I'll tell him!
The boy meant business but didn't want to step forward and snatch the jamun from his brother, presumably because he knew the little fellow would put it in his mouth. The little boy held the jamun close to his lips, measuring his brother's threat. I felt like interceding in his favour but then thought better of it, for I didn't want to risk the jamun-seller's wrath. The little boy put the jamun back in the basket and began to whimper.
—Someday you'll be my undoing! the boy exclaimed.
—Is he your little brother?
—Yes.
His tone seemed to have added: And I'm ashamed of him.
I stepped forward, bent down, patted the little boy's head, and said—You're very fond of jamuns, aren't you?
He stopped crying and snuggled close to his brother. He couldn't have been more than four; his big brother's age was difficult to guess.
The jamun-seller returned, examined the baskets, then the boys, and last of all me. He smiled. I felt like baring my teeth for his inspection but did not.
—At this time of the day the buses are always late.
He seemed to have decided to reward me for my vigilance. I looked at my watch. There was still a lot of time. I cursed myself

for having come too early.

—You want me to get some water for sprinkling?

—I'll go too.

The little boy looked determined to do something this time. The man broke into a laugh. The boys dashed off to the shacks.

—They hang around me all the time.

I paid him no attention.

—The big one is really smart.

I kept quiet.

—How old do you think he is?

I didn't want to make a guess and was glad at the arrival of a couple with a child.

—How long have you been waiting, mister?

The man's tone was that of a born bus passenger.

—For ages!

—I told you we won't get a bus at this time of day.

The man's wife sounded like a born nag.

—It will be along soon, I consoled them.

They paid me no attention.

—I'm going to Kashmere Gate; where are you going?

—To Mori Gate. To my sister-in-law's place. Her eldest son is going to have his first haircut.

I decided not to promote the conversation any further.

—What time is it? The man had asked that question out of sheer national habit.

—Ten-past-two.

—I want jamuns, I want jamuns, their son began to sing.

—Lovely dark jamuns! Very cheap! Lovely dark jamuns!

—Lovely dark jamuns! Very cheap!

The boy's chant was more musical than his bread-giver's. He had already come back with a canister full of water and was sprinkling the ground around the jamun-seller's throne. The little boy had brought a bundle of green leaves.

—I carried these, he told the jamun-seller.

—Good, the man said in a casual tone as he opened the bundle and soaked the leaves in water. Then he started to make two pyramids of jamuns on a wooden plank that the boy had put in front of him. One pyramid was dark purple, the other light.

—I want jamuns, I want jamuns!

—Lovely dark jamuns! Very cheap!

This time the little boy had added his chant to his brother's.

—Give him twenty paise worth.

—Only twenty paise worth!

The man ignored the jamun-seller's derision. The jamun-seller salted a few jamuns, tossed them around in his clay pot, and handed them to the whimpering child. The little boy sneaked up to the child. The woman picked up her son and started feeding him. The son didn't want to be fed but the woman was a born feeder. The little boy stared at the woman for a while before slinking back to his brother.

—Lovely dark jamuns! Delicious jamuns! Very cheap jamuns!

The boy seemed to be enjoying his chant. The woman smiled at him appreciatively.

—A smart boy, the man remarked.

—I wish this idiot of ours was half as smart, said the woman and kissed her idiot.

—Where have the customers gone today? Shall I shout louder? And then, without waiting for an answer, he started singing louder—O these lovely dark jamuns! O these black clouds! O these heat-killing jamuns!

This time, however, he seemed out of tune. As he raised his voice, his throat became taut and the veins around his neck became as thick as the little boy's little finger. The jamun-seller kept busy with his pyramids. Every few minutes he too cried out his wares but his cries seemed self-consciously aware of the inferiority of his vocal cords. The little boy had started doing all sorts of interesting things. Every time the boy chanted, he joined him. Then he made a face like he'd just eaten a sour jamun. Then he involuntarily stretched out his hand to the two pyramids. The jamun-seller pushed his hand back without looking at him. If he was not attentive, the boy checked his brother.

Then a bus came along. It wasn't my bus. The couple with their idiot got on the bus. A few people got off it. Two of them, both big women, walked toward the pyramids. One of them wanted the inferior variety, the other went for the superior. The jamun-seller assured them that all his jamuns were juicy. The women ignored his assurances and made their own selections. I amused myself watching them. As they walked away, the little boy followed them a few steps. Then he walked back and started staring at the jamuns. His mouth moved around imaginary jamuns. A few minutes later a man came along with his little son holding him by his index finger. He bought two rupees worth of jamuns and they walked away. The little boy followed them too for a few steps before slouching back to the baskets.

—Lovely dark beauties! Very cheap! Darker than clouds! Very cheap!

A bunch of young boys appeared from nowhere, bought lots of jamuns, sat down near the baskets, and started eating them in a determined way.

The little boy was in great torment now. He looked, now at the jamuns, now at the jamun-seller, and all of a sudden his entire little body began to itch. Once or twice he caught his brother's eye and made an imploring little pout. He looked very cute as he did that.

—We'll have a crowd of customers when the next bus comes, the boy said to the jamun-seller.

The jamun-seller looked at me and winked. I didn't know what he was trying to tell me.

—I think we'll sell everything by the evening, the boy went on.

The jamun-seller smiled. His wink was less ugly than his smile.

When those young boys left, the boy whispered to the jamun-seller—Now will you give us some?

—Of course, I will, but let's sell some first. You can't be hungry already; you just had your food!

The jamun-seller had raised his voice apparently for my benefit. I paid him no attention.

—I want some now, the little boy whimpered.

Nobody paid him any attention. Just then a tonga came along at a pace slow enough for the driver to be tempted by the juicy jamuns. He parked his tonga and ordered half a pound of jamuns.

The Stone of a Jamun

He sat down close to the jamun-seller's throne and started eating with loud relish. He was toothless, so he had to roll and squeeze each jamun with his gums many times before he was done with it. He spat each stone in a different direction. The little boy stared at his mouth.

Then two young men came along and asked the tonga man whether he wanted to go to Connaught Place. He got up promptly and put the rest of the jamuns beside the driver's seat. One of the young men asked the other—How about some jamuns? The other said—How about them! I hear they're good for digestion! The boy set up an instant chant—Lovely jamuns! Good for digestion! The young men laughed. Then one of them ordered three rupees' worth. The other shouted—Are you crazy! The jamun-seller quickly weighed three rupees' worth of jamuns, salted them, shook them vigorously in his clay pot, and handed them to his customers. He was all ugly smiles now.

After the tonga had left the boy whispered to the man—Now will you give us some?

—Look, boy, don't you pester me! I told you I'd give you some, but first let's sell some! I'm not eating any, am I?

The jamun-seller transferred some more jamuns on to the pyramids and sprinkled water over them. They glistened in the sun. As he ran his hands up and down the two pyramids, he quietly picked up a couple of the jamuns and tossed them into his mouth, like digestive pills.

I looked at my watch. I was growing old, standing by those cloud-dark jamuns. The boy sat close to his brother now, both of them staring at the jamuns helplessly. When the little boy moved his mouth around his imaginary jamuns, his brother did the same.

—Jamuns! Cheap jamuns! Eat jamuns!

The jamun-seller's voice was so unattractive that one would feel like spitting the jamuns out rather than eating them.

Another bus came but it wasn't my bus.

—Look, boy, get up and start shouting! Don't you see the crowd getting off this bus!

The boy got up and started shouting. It so happened that almost everyone who got off the bus bought some jamuns. A couple of them tried to strike a deal for one full basket but the jamun-seller didn't want to sell wholesale.

After everybody had left, the boy said—Now will you give me some?

At first the man tried to stare him into silence. Then he looked at me, smiled, winked, and said—Hold it, boy, hold it! Impatience never pays.

—I want some now, the little boy got up, stamped his feet, and repeated his demand defiantly.

—At least give him a couple. Please! the boy pleaded on behalf of his brother.

The man took out a crumpled paper bag from underneath one of the baskets. He took out three jamuns from the bag and gave them to the little boy. These jamuns were neither dark purple nor light purple. They were of some unknown colour, and they looked like crushed beetles. The brothers looked at them with considerable scepticism before the little boy put one in his mouth and made a wry face. He offered one to his brother, who took it, but when he thought the jamun-seller wasn't looking, he threw it away. The man saw that jamun as it fell at my feet. He recognized it and shouted in an indignant tone—Hey you! Who do you think you are! A nabob! Now pick that up and eat it.

The boy was terribly embarrassed. He hesitated, but his little brother ran forward, picked the jamun up, wiped it on his bare belly, and put it in his mouth.

The jamun-seller winked me a smile. Just then a bus came along from the other direction. It was my bus going the wrong way. Several passengers got off it.

—Look, boy, get up and start shouting.

The boy got up and started shouting. But there was no music in his chant. Even then quite a few people crossed the street over to our side. Maybe jamuns are the real weakness of all bus passengers, especially of women. They love to nibble and munch and smack their lips. It must be their biology. Or some mean streak in them. I amused myself with several similar observations. Clichés really. Quite a crowd had gathered around the jamun-seller, who was taking full advantage of the situation, weighing less and palming off inferior jamuns at the price of the superior variety. He was about to run out of green leaves. So he shouted to the boy to run and get some. The boy ran off. The little boy remained where he was. When the boy came back, there were still a few customers left. He got into the act and cried—Lovely cloud-dark jamuns! Black beauties! Very cheap!

—You've got a smart boy, one of the customers remarked to the jamun-seller.

The jamun-seller sent me a conspiratorial smile. I turned it down.

—Lovely jamuns! Made specially for old women! Eat them!

At this, everybody, including the jamun-seller, laughed. The little boy, however, did not. He was looking up at the mouths of the jamun-eaters, his own mouth hanging open. I saw a tall man holding a jamun in his hand, aiming it at the little boy's mouth. The little boy opened his mouth wide. The tall man popped the jamun into his own mouth and laughed and left. The big boy sounded tired. His neck seemed swollen with shouting. Then he saw his brother running after the tall man, begging for a jamun. He ordered him to come back. The little boy came back and started staring at the jamuns.

—Please give us some now.

The jamun-seller flared up—Look, boy, haven't I told you not to pester me when the customers are there? Don't you know any manners?

The boy looked really embarrassed now.

—Some wretches get addicted to beggary, said a middle-aged ogress and waddled away with her jamuns.

The boy was trying to catch the man's eye.

—Well, here you are then! The man took a handful of colourless jamuns from his special bag and gave them to the boy.—Now you better perk up and start shouting!

The boy didn't perk up but he shouted all right. By now a few people had joined me. Some of them wanted me to tell what time it was, others wanted to know how long I had been waiting there, still others wondered whether my watch was correct. I had too much company now. I took a vow not to wear a watch in public.

Jamuns had suddenly gone out of favour.

—How about now? There are no customers now. Please give us a few good ones now.

The boy's voice was so soft that even I heard it with some effort. The jamun-seller paid him no attention and set up an appeal of his own—Come, all you jamun-eaters! Eat my lovely jamuns!

—You promised, whispered the boy.

But before the man could either redeem or debase himself further in my eyes, he was besieged by a woman and her four brats.

—Welome, welcome!

The jamun-seller was all ugly grins. I thought he perhaps knew that woman, or else had recognized her as an endlessly fertile mother of many more future jamun-eaters. The woman sat down close to the pyramids. The little boy also moved closer to them. He'd already finished those special jamuns. Now he gazed hungrily at the mouths of that woman's four children. The big boy was also staring greedily at the jamuns now.

—How much?

—What's the rate?

After a bit of bargaining the jamun-seller agreed to lower his rate, specially for that woman. She ordered some jamuns for each of her children and herself. The little boy had by now taken a position along with the woman's brats. As the jamun-seller handed jamuns to each child, the little boy stretched out his hand. I had expected him to do this. After having ignored him four times, the jamun-seller searched that bag for special jamuns, but there weren't any there. He selected a special jamun from one of the baskets and threw it to the little boy, who caught it expertly and put it in his mouth. I was waiting for him to put his hand out for more. But the little boy knew better. He was gazing at the mouths of those brats. And moving his mouth over his imaginary jamuns. Soon he began to drool. The string of his purple saliva stretched down to his bare belly. The jamun-seller was busy shaping his pyramids into purple perfection. The little boy's brother too had started staring at the brats' mouths and moving his mouth over his imaginary jamuns. The two brothers opened and shut their mouths more or less simultaneously; they swallowed their saliva as if it

The Stone of a Jamun

was jamun juice. The big boy had his arm around the little boy's shoulders. I saw a string of saliva coming out of his mouth; before it could break, he slurped it back into his mouth. I was nauseated. I put my hands in my pockets and counted my coins. I had just enough for bus fare and two cigarettes. I was disgusted with myself.

—Please give us some now!

It was the boy. I didn't like his meek tone. His brother was still staring at the purple mouths of those brats and eating his own imaginary jamuns.

—No more now!

The jamun-seller sounded very decisive. I saw a bus approaching. It looked like my bus. I hadn't decided what I should do with the money I'd reserved for two cigarettes. My hands were still in my pocket, fondling my meagre funds, as I walked to the edge of the road. I turned around and saw the two brothers sitting close to the jamuns and staring at them. I had half a hope that they would start cursing the jamun-seller. I had half an intention that, if they spoke for themselves, I would too, even if it meant missing my bus, which was getting close to the stop. And then I heard them crying. Both of them had their hands out.

—Please give us some!

I was annoyed. I hadn't expected the big boy to break down that easily. I should have known better. I took my hands out of my pockets. Then I saw that the little boy had started picking up the stones of the jamuns. Before I boarded my bus I heard one of the customers saying to his companion—Jamun is a wonderful fruit, you know; even the stone of a jamun is good; it's the best remedy for impotence, you know.

The Voice-Robber

Just as I stepped out, I saw him standing near the gate, staring at my house. I paid him little attention. Some men are fond of ogling at other men's wives till they reach a certain age after which they develop a fondness for ogling at their houses. He is one of those, I thought, or perhaps he is just waiting for someone, or perhaps he has stopped to catch his breath and is feeding his envy by admiring my house. Some men are fond of envying other men for their wives till they reach a certain age after which they start envying them for their houses.

But for my capricious dog, I would have ignored the man and started my stroll along one of the few fixed routes I take, slouching in my fixed manner, without exchanging a look or word with that stranger. People living in big cities rarely exchange words or looks with strangers. They avoid any kind of contact with strangers. But for my wayward dog, I too would have avoided that stranger, particularly because my hair stood on end when I looked at him a little carefully while pulling my dog away. According to the normal canine practice, my dog should have barked at him,

The Voice-Robber

particularly after it had smelled my fear. But then all dogs do not always behave according to the dog book. My dog came to an absolute stop near that man in a manner that suggested it was offering him an explanation or an apology on my behalf. My dog, like everybody else's dog, often gives me surprises that please as well as irritate me. But that day I was only irritated at its behaviour. I gave it a savage pull, gnashed my teeth, and hissed its name with an excessive fierceness, but the wretch was unmoved. Holding aloft its snout, it sniffed the air around that stranger with an intensity that suggested it had discovered an aeons-old affinity or smell that it had to investigate and make its own before moving on. That stranger was now looking into my dog's eyes in a manner that made me suspect he was casting a spell on my beast and, through it, on me. The nameless fear that had gripped me a little earlier had decreased a little by now. I had swept my eyes over him when he was not looking. He was an awkward old man of my age. He had a few day's grisly growth on his face. His clothes were shabby, his chappals loose, his teeth dirty, and his eyes desolate. As I gave another savage pull to my dog, the man spoke out abruptly—Not so hard, old man, or do you really want to break the poor pet's neck?

My hair stood on end once again. My grip on the leash became unfirm, I began to sweat profusely. The voice that had come out of the stranger's mouth was mine. He has robbed me of my voice through some sorcery, I thought. My dog is smelling my voice in him, I thought. Now the dog was looking at me, asking me why I was so scared. I gave it a pull on the sly but it didn't budge. I didn't want to open my mouth. I feared that I would not produce any sound. I also feared that the sound of my voice would be utterly unfamiliar to me and that the stranger would laugh and the sound of that laughter would also be mine. These were insane fears but I could not shake them off. Just then I heard him say—Come on, then; your dog wants me to join you in your stroll; I'll do that to please the beast. This time around also, he had spoken in my voice.

I don't know even now what I should have done then. I don't know what anyone else in my place would have done. But I started walking along with him obediently while my dog danced around us with unconcealed relief. That man seemed to know the route I would take that day for my stroll. Even if he hadn't, there wouldn't have been any problem because my dog had started dragging me as it cantered ahead of us, looking like a miniature black horse. After we had gone a short distance, the stranger quietly snatched the leash from my hand. It looked as if he had taken hold of the reins. My hands were empty now and my mind was filled with apprehensions. My dog dragged the stranger now. It seemed to belong to him. It appeared as if it was keen on taking him to a spot both of them knew and I didn't. I lagged behind them, and the distance between us seemed to be increasing very fast every moment. Then, all of a sudden, I had an eerie feeling that the ground was literally slipping from under my feet, as if my dog and the stranger were moving away on a fast train, while I stood on a deserted platform. I wanted to call my dog back, but I feared no voice would come out of my mouth, or, if one did, it would not be mine. I held my tongue even as I kept lagging behind them. Neither of them looked back even once. I was much pained by my dog's infidelity. The distance between us was increasing so fast that I could hardly see them.

When they disappeared into the dusty distance, I turned around and started walking back to my house, thanking God that the stranger had made away with my dog and not with my wife or my house. At that time I forgot that he had also robbed me of my voice, perhaps permanently.

My Effigy

Finally, one day, toward the end of a venomous quarrel, I said to her in a cold sullen voice: Look here, my dear, I've had it; you do not approve of anything I do or say; you are always bursting with rage or lying away from me like a slab of ice; you insist on digging out dead issues so that you can say you can't stand their stink; you hit so hard that even a boulder would crumble under your blows; your eyes no less than your words accuse me of being a liar, a wastrel, a lecher, a drunkard, a glutton, a maniac, a sycophant, psychopath, a self-server, a vulgarian, a demon, and you alone know what else; you gnash your teeth ten times a day and wonder how you've put up with me all these years; you threaten to leave me for Vrindavan every other evening . . . look here, my dear, things have gone too far, but I wish to offer you a solution, which may still salvage our relationship and see us through the rest of our appointed days in this vale of fears, provided you agree to act on it, if only on a trial basis, for a few days, for I am told this device has gained an immense currency in the developed world—yes, yes, I called it my solution for the sake of brevity and convenience, but actually it is an ancient remedy that has now come into vogue after centuries of neglect—give it a chance and you'll be giving peace a chance; well, then, the remedy is that you ask someone to make you an effigy of me, warts and all; or if you like I can get it done for you; you put that effigy in a place that is convenient so that you can keep hitting it as you come and go—with your fists or feet or even with a whip—and you can also keep spitting at it whenever the desire possesses you; this will provide you a release for all your fury and give you a more genuine satisfaction than you get now, for I won't be able to retaliate, particularly when you hit me when I am not there or when I am asleep; I've heard a lot about the effectiveness of this remedy or whatever you'd like to call it; I've heard, in fact, that millions of marriages have been saved by this magical method.

I'd offered this suggestion in an outburst of irony, hoping that it would infuriate or freeze her. She said nothing at the time. A few days later I discovered that she had acquired a rather well-stuffed effigy that looked more or less like me. Now that effigy is firmly planted in the little corridor connecting her room with mine. She hits it with her feet or fists as she goes about her business, day and night, whenever the impulse seizes her. She hasn't taken the whip to it so far. She spits at it even as she showers curses whenever the spirit moves her. In the beginning she did it only when my back was turned, now she doesn't mind my presence. She is very happy now, at peace with herself and me, all sweetness and light, bursting with zest for life. But I am absolutely deflated. I've begun to despise myself. My body seems alien to me, my mind a mess—I've become my effigy, battered and bruised, covered with spit, pierced by curses.

The Soul of Darkness

There is a narrow dungeon in my house. It is cluttered with all kinds of junk I have saved all my life and forgotten about. And it is also cluttered with darkness—the useless darkness I have saved all my life and forgotten about, as well as the useless darkness that oozes out of every day that passes. The door of this dungeon has been eaten at several places by time and darkness. That is why, perhaps, it stands always ajar in a way that suggests to me that the dungeon emits darkness and swallows it simultaneously. The light bulb in the dungeon burnt out years ago. Until a few years ago, I used to play with the idea of changing the bulb, but never got round to doing it because of my fear of darkness. Then, gradually, it started seeming proper to me that the light bulb in the dungeon should remain burnt out forever. Until a few years ago, I used to squeeze into the dungeon, every now and then, and potter around—in a manner of speaking—arranging and disarranging the long-forgotten junk, staring at some selected items in the staggering glow of a candle. Until a few years ago, I used to make feeble resolutions about throwing everything out into the street. Then, gradually, I got rid of this foolish habit. Now the very thought of entering that dungeon fills me with consternation.

Every now and then I throw some new piece of junk into it with a fury that would suggest I am delivering a blow to the darkness stored inside. Until a few years ago, on some selected days, I used to enter the dungeon before the crack of dawn and somehow sit down, naked, my eyes closed, my body motionless in a yogic posture, like a man praying in the dark to the dark. I felt as if I was on the verge of establishing an ineffable rapport with the darkness stored in the dungeon. I also felt I was on the verge of doing nothing of the sort, that all that had happened was that I had managed to snatch a false sense of security from that darkness. Then, gradually, I dropped this stupid practice. These days, sometimes, just as I am about to step out for my morning stroll, I stop short in front of the dungeon door, that always stands ajar, like a man seized by uncertainty at a forked path. During that brief seizure, I am assailed by many dark and beautiful longings. I keep playing with them during my morning stroll.

This morning also, I was seized by uncertainty wrapped in dark and beautiful longings as I stopped short before the dungeon door. I should have overcome the seizure, as I always do, and moved out of the house for my morning stroll, but I pushed the dungeon door open and stepped in. Instead of arranging or disarranging the barely visible junk or stripping myself naked and sitting down somehow in a prayer-like posture, I started prodding the darkness with my walking-stick in a manner that would suggest I was provoking a corpse or a demon or a serpent into life. Soon I was almost dancing in furious ecstasy in that narrow space, even as I beat that darkness and that junk I had saved all my life and forgotten. I made fancy fencing passes, parodying a master swordsman with my little walking-stick. For a while nothing happened. Then, suddenly, an invisible hand snatched my stick and started giving me a thrashing the likes of which I never got even in my naughty childhood. Anyone else in my place would have been finished; I didn't even lose consciousness. I am lying now in a nursing home, recovering from those blows, experiencing them again and again with perverse pleasure.

The Fourth Window

This room of mine is like the head of this house. It has many windows; so many, in fact, that if all of them were open at the same time, it would change into a wind-room and I into a fluttering piece of blank paper. This house is very tall—like a pole stuck in the sky. I have never seen all the windows of this room open at the same time. I have never tried to open all of them. The truth, perhaps, is that even if I tried to open all of them I would not be able to do so. My arms are feeble, my will-power dead. Even so, I am never quite free of the anxiety that some evening, in my desperation, I shall smash these windows open and flutter awhile like a piece of blank paper in the wind that rushes in, and then expire. This anxiety may also be my desire. My desires come to me in the guise of anxieties now, my anxieties in the guise of desires. No anxiety chills my blood now, no desire warms it. This assertion is false, for whenever I see myself fluttering like a piece of blank paper, my blood freezes at first and then begins to boil, and I break into a laughter that is as pure as that of a corpse—soundless and endless.

These days I spend a part of every evening in this room, alone, after my evening stroll. I feel alarmed as well as reassured by the height of this house. The source of my alarm and reassurance is the same: one of these evenings I shall open one of the windows and hurl myself into the well of darkness and no one will ever know. I have experienced this ecstasy in my dreams a few times; I doubt if I shall ever do so in reality.

On some evenings I do open three of these windows but I seldom open all three of them at the same time. Whenever an impulse makes me do that, I see myself divided into three parts. Then I have to resort to all sorts of occult devices, chant all sorts of mantras, in order to overcome the dread induced by my self-division. Those devices are not occult, those mantras are not mantras. If some invisible observer were to watch me in that condition, he would conclude some maniac was going to pieces because of some mistake in his meditation. I know there is no invisible observer watching me when I am in that condition, but I can't quite get rid of the fear that there is one. Finally I am able to overcome that dread only by somehow putting myself together and closing the three windows. My palms and fingers are lacerated in the process.

Then I fold my lacerated hands and stand before that fourth closed window which I cannot open, but about which I have this blind faith that, some evening, in answer to the mute prayers of my lacerated hands, it will open of itself. I have a suspicion that I lacerate my hands only in order to make their mute prayers more effective, hoping that the fourth window will open and release me from this room. My faith in the fourth is in proportion to my ignorance about it. That is why, perhaps, I do not know how to open it. That is why, perhaps, I hope it will open of itself some day and release me from this room.

My first window opens on a narrow playground surrounded by narrow houses. The playground looks like a common courtyard. There I see a few half-clad urchins throwing crumpled balls of waste paper up in the air or trying to fly some ill-made kites or straining to catch the hornets buzzing over little pools of stagnant water. I keep looking for myself among these urchins. Little mounds of dirt and garbage scattered about look like tiny graves. In the raw darkness of the evening, these graves are sometimes beautiful, and I keep staring at them. After a while I hear mothers calling their kids by name, urging them to come in, for the darkness is getting thick. I try to catch my name among those names, my mother's voice among those voices. Then I imagine all those names are mine, all those voices are my mother's. The scene undergoes an abrupt change. I see the inside of a narrow house, drowned in darkness, glutted with smoke. I see two smoky figures, standing face to face, growling at each other, ready to pounce—a scene out of my recurring nightmares.

My second window opens on a spruce park. A few old men and women are engaged in calisthenics. I look for myself among them. I hear babies and the chirping of birds. I see a few crisp nannies and a few brisk dogs. Then the scene undergoes an abrupt change. I see several large houses. I see an old person or two lying about forlorn in every house. I see their wrinkles, their longings enmeshed in those wrinkles. I hear their regrets. I hear their deaths. I feel as if I had seen myself in various forms.

My third window opens on solid darkness, soon broken by many emerging creatures that are neither human nor unhuman, neither birds nor beasts, neither male nor female, neither happy nor unhappy, neither familiar nor unfamiliar. I see no house. I hear no voice. This scene undergoes no change. My dread goes on mounting. When it is beyond my bearing, everything gets lost in the solid darkness once again.

The sights I see through the first window give me pain as well as pleasure; the sights through the second window only revulsion; the sights through the third only dread.

I do not know when and how the fourth window will open and on what sights. I do not know how to open it. My blind faith says it will open some evening of itself in answer to the mute entreaties of my lacerated hands. And that it will open on nothing, nothing at all. And after I have had a glimpse of that void, I shall be released from this room.

These days I spend every evening waiting for that release.

The Thieves' Thief

I

Every evening as I sit alone in this room surveying my day and dread, my fingers groping for my failing pulse, I am visited by a thief. Before his visitation, my survey and pulse seem equally lifeless; the day with all its trivial mishaps yields no new meaning, no new gloom; the dread offers no new insight, no new light; I feel like laughing at my absurd endurance. Then, just as I am about to go beyond my day and dread and cast a cold eye on my entire existence, he comes in, and I come alive as if I had seen a serpent.

II

I see no crack either in the bolted door or the smooth ceiling. I hear no squeak from any window. I do not hear either his footsteps or the hiss of his breathing. But I know for sure he has come in. He is formless. He is the ideal thief. The thieves' thief. I am convinced about his arrival by the startled silence of my body. It would seem my body had seen him but not I. I feel envious of my body. I feel like reducing me to my body. Then this desire seems redundant. What am I if not my body?

III

Perhaps that thief visits me only to tell me what I am. No, not to tell me but to force me to face the question. No, thieves do not visit people to tell them anything or to force them to face any question. They come to steal.

IV

It may well be that he comes to steal my laughter. My laughter is my only attainment. If that goes, I go. He must be aware of this. Even a common thief is fairly well-informed about his prospective victims. He is an uncommon thief. He is the thieves' thief. I am sure he knows I am able to endure my day and dread only because of my laughter. It may well be that he is an assassin disguised as a thief. I shall speak to him one of these evenings. Take my body away, I shall say, but spare me my laughter, for my laughter is my soul. I have never actually said anything to him so far but I am sure he knows all I want to say to him.

V

One of these evenings I shall say to him: What kind of a thief are you that you come here every evening but do not take anything away? Is there nothing here worth your stealing? Then why do you come? Because you think I may have acquired some new trash? I swear to you I shall never bring in anything now. I want to see this room absolutely empty. I know that as long as I am here this room will not be absolutely empty. That is why I implore you to take me away. I know I am of no use to you. I know I have not been of any use to myself. . . . I never go beyond this point in my imaginary colloquy with him.

VI

One of these evenings I shall put him to shame: Look here, you are a thief, a thief of thieves, thieving is your dharma; if you do not see anything worth stealing here, if you really think I am of no use to you, why do you bother me every evening? Why don't you steal something? Are you afraid I shall cry Thief! I promise you I shall never do that. Never.

VII

I shall tell him one of these evenings: Look, if I am of no use to you, why don't you rob me of my desires, or my memories, or my memory? Perhaps you will say you are a thief, not a do-gooder. Why don't you say it then? I would like to hear your voice for once. I am not even sure whether you are real or unreal. Perhaps you do not even exist. If you do, reveal yourself to me.

VIII

Every now and then I am seized by the suspicion that he does not come here to steal but to hide things he has stolen from elsewhere. Then, after he leaves, I glare into every nook and corner of this room. I sweep it again and again, I sift the dirt by using a sieve. I do not find a thing that was not already here. But I cannot get rid of the suspicion that he has left something somewhere in the room, something that is invisible, like himself, and dangerous.

IX

Every now and then I am seized by the suspicion that he is not a thief, I am; that he is the owner of this room and drops in every evening to evict me, but then he spares me out of pity. When I am in the grip of this suspicion, my laughter loses its power and I feel like shouting at him: Where will I go if you evict me from here? To another hell?

X

Sometimes I try to draw some solace from the thought that nobody comes into this room, that nobody goes out of it—nobody, that is, except me—that the thief does not exist, that he is a figment of my imagination. But even this thought does not give me any permanent peace of mind.

An Evensong

The waitresses and the woman they worked for were Japanese but the patrons appeared to be from other lands and unknown to one another. They sat at small separate tables, sipping their drinks like a medicine that seemed to increase their anguish. Their heads were bent, their eyes lightless. I sat in a corner from where, on lifting my head slightly, I could see everyone in the bar. My eyes too were lightless. I too was sipping my drink like a medicine.

I had stopped in that city for two days and that was my first evening there. I could not shake off the impression that I had been there before, that I had spent an evening there in that very ambience, in that very mood, in the midst of almost those very people. In order to gather some supporting evidence for this insistent impression, I lifted my head slightly every few minutes and cast my lightless eyes around—at the dour proprietress, the winsome waitresses, the grim patrons imbibing their medicine, the decor of the bar, the spectacular array of the bottles. My anguish lay inside me like a blue rock. I drank steadily, waiting for it to start throbbing.

I had nothing to do in that city. I did not know anyone there. That was why I had stopped there. I was wondering how and why I had strayed into that bar where, except for the owner and the waitresses, everybody appeared to be from some other country, sitting alone, sipping their drinks like a medicine that seemed to be increasing their anguish. I was also wondering why my anguish lay inside me like a blue rock impervious to the medicine I was imbibing. I was also wondering when that blue rock would begin to throb. I would have wondered some more but just then a woman walked over to my table from hers, carrying her glass, and sat down. She did not ask me whether she could join me. She looked deep into my eyes and beckoned me to raise my glass, which I did obediently. After we had taken a sip each, we put our glasses down solemnly. A little light had come into my eyes with the coming of that woman. She had an ordinary face and extraordinary eyes. Her soul seemed to be radiating from them. I imagined that, by kissing her eyes, even a perennially peaceless person like me would become profoundly peaceful. I imagined other things also.

It must have been because of her reassuring eyes that I burst into a monologue in my language which, I was sure, she did not know: I have this bad habit; every evening after I have imbibed a certain amount of my medicine, I start licking the salt of my failures; it is like an animal licking its sores; I like unsuccessful people; they are my kin; they have a special odour; I hate the greasiness of success; I believe that every success is ill-gotten, that every successful person is more or less dishonest, that every success is built on several others' failures; I do not get any peace from this belief; I have doubts about its truth; I am convinced I am unsuccessful in my own eyes as well as in others'; I am not proud of this habit of licking the salt of my unsuccess every evening but I cannot shed this addiction; I don't even want to; I am afraid I won't know how to endure my evenings without it; I am one of those absolute failures who cherish no illusions, give themselves no concession, give others no concession, draw no satisfaction from any success;

my anguish lies inside me like a blue rock; every evening I drink steadily until it begins to throb; when it does, I burst into a monologue; I do not drink while I deliver my monologue; I resume drinking after I am done; but after a point I can neither drink nor lick the salt of my unsuccess; normally, after that point, I fall asleep or perhaps pass out; one of these days I shall pass away after that point; I do not draw any satisfaction from this. . . .

My companion held my hand in hers. Her pressure assured me she had understood me perfectly even though she did not know my language. I pressed back my thanks and also the suggestion that, unless she objected, our hands should remain interlocked for a while more. The blue rock of my anguish was throbbing well. That woman was the same age as I. I am always aware of my age. In the evening this awareness becomes more intense. It warms me up a bit and reduces the terror of the evening. If that woman had not walked over to my table, I would have delivered my monologue in an inaudible mumble. I became instantly convinced that everybody sitting in that bar was from a different country, spoke a different language. I had no basis for this instant conviction. Perhaps, in order to acquire some basis, I raised my head and looked around. Some of the people had left their tables and gone over to other tables. Those who still sat alone struck me as belonging to a breed higher than mine. I would have mused some more but just then my companion started whispering her monologue in her language, which I did not know but could understand perfectly. She was saying: I have this bad habit; every evening after I have imbibed a certain amount of my medicine, I start licking the salt of my failures; it is like an animal. . . .

As she approached the end of her monologue, I pressed her hand and assured her that I had understood her perfectly. She pressed back her thanks.

After that we could have spent that night in her hotel or mine. We did not do that. We pressed each other's hands for one last time, got up, and walked out of that bar. I kissed her eyes. She kissed mine. Then she went to her hotel, I to mine.

An Evening with Bhookh Kumari

I was out on my favourite deserted road for my evening stroll. My pace was slow, my mind sad. I was taking long breaths in order to empty my mind and smiling ruefully at my failures. One long strip of the sky was smeared with a pale redness that was fading fast, like my smile. The evening had not let her hair down yet. The road lay spread before me like a crushed cobra. I was trampling it and myself, like a homeless old man. I had not yet reached the boulder where I usually sit for a spell and peer down at the shanties glimmering far below while my imagination hovers around them like a pigeon with broken wings. I often feel like standing on that boulder and taking a plunge into that network of glimmering shanties every evening. I have never done it. This impulse does not strike me with any terror or horror. It is one of my numerous stillborn impulses.

I rarely go beyond that boulder in my evening strolls along my favourite road. Every old idler has a tree or ditch or turning or boulder or some such spot beyond which he does not normally stray but beyond which he always wants to go. That evening, however, I saw someone else sitting on my boulder, and I strayed beyond it because I did not want to sit on it next to any person. Had

I noticed the usurper in time, I might have turned around. But I was slouching along with my head down, and it was only after I had reached the boulder that I realized my place on it had been taken by someone else. Turning around abruptly did not seem right to me. Looking straight at that little figure also did not seem right to me. A relentless censor always lurks in my mind, telling me what is not right. Every evening I try in vain to throw it out of my mind. That evening also, I tried and failed. I stopped short near the boulder, then moved on, at a slightly quicker pace. I intended to look back a little later in order to be sure I had not imagined that little figure on the boulder. If it was still there, I would pretend I had just thought of an important reason to turn around and rush homeward. But I had barely gone beyond that boulder when everything began to assume another aspect. The idea of looking back got lost somewhere. I started walking briskly, breathing freely. I felt suddenly more alert, more alive. I stopped trampling myself. A smile bloomed on my lips. It seemed by going beyond that boulder I had entered another sphere. I was astonished at the change in my mood. I started walking with my chest thrown out, my arms swaying in long sweeps, like a retired army officer or a resolute Arya Samajist. My carriage is even otherwise quite good, better than my age and appearance would suggest. I tame it deliberately during my evening stroll in order to descend into what I self-derisively call my interior space, and to empty my mind. It is a different matter that instead of achieving that descent, I begin to trample myself.

My mood, however, did not last very long. All of a sudden I was seized by the fear that someone was following me. I am familiar with this fear. I am often seized by it, especially on deserted roads, in the evening, when the day is about to breathe its last. My blood freezes and my ears turn red whenever this happens. I want to turn around and see but do not dare. Generally this fear leaves me after a while. It is like an epileptic fit—unpredictable and awful. As long as I am in its grip, I am tense with the apprehension that the phantom following me will pounce upon me any second and finish me off. It has not happened so far, but I cannot say it never will. That evening also, my body was all ready for a fatal assault

An Evening with Bhookh Kumari

from behind. I could hear the gradually rising sound of my pursuer's footsteps. My desire to turn around and see was killed by my old dread that, if I saw no one behind me, I would go mad. At first I thought I might be hearing my own footsteps but I knew I was not. So I started waiting for the unpredictable end of my seizure. Generally, when I get soaking wet with perspiration, the pursuing footsteps start fading out, and I come to know that my fit, or whatever it is, is about to end. But that evening my body remained dry even though that shuffling sound was now very close, as if someone was almost upon my heels. Just as I started thinking that, my phantom pursuer was at last about to catch up with me. I heard an impish voice—Please turn around now, for I am tired.

I was not startled. It was the voice of a raw young girl. It reassured me instead of frightening me. The sound of mischief in it was sweet to my ears. My fear vanished. I stopped. She also stopped. For a few seconds I stood with my back toward her, hoping she would step forward and face me. When she neither stepped forward nor uttered another word, I realized she was adamantly waiting for me to turn around and would not make her next move until then. She seemed to be a person of principles, in spite of her raw youth. I rather liked that.

She was barefoot and bareheaded. And she was smiling. She had on a dirty blue dress that barely reached her bruised knees. In her tangled unwashed hair she had a red ribbon. Her smile too was red but her lips were parched, her cheeks streaked with dirt. Her hands were interlocked behind her head as she swayed on her bare feet. Her wrists were thin, her big eyes bright. It is because of the brightness in her eyes, I thought, I can see her so clearly in the dark. All my apprehensions had already disappeared.

—Who are you? I asked her tenderly.

She mentioned her name, on hearing which I was amused, surprised, and pained.

—*Bhookh Ki Mari*? What kind of a name is that?

The girl laughed.

—*Bhookh Ki Mari!* Is that what you heard? Wonderful!

I realized I had made a mistake. I started laughing with her. I heard the evening laughing in her laughter; she must have heard the night laughing in mine.

—It's not *Bhookh Ki Mari*, she corrected me, it is *Bhookh Kumari*.

My laughter ended abruptly. I began to brood. I did not quite know what I was brooding about. Keeping quiet, however, did not seem quite right to me.

—Your name is unusual, I said.

—But my form is not, she rejoined.

I was impressed. A smart girl! But she shouldn't be out so late in the evening and that too so far from town. I shall walk her back home.

—Yes, your form is not, I pretended to agree with her.

—I know all about you, she said, where you live, what you....

—Really? I interrupted her.

—By God! she said in English.

I was amused but also a bit alarmed. I brushed aside the alarm and said—What are you doing here so late in the evening?

—Talking to you, she laughed.

This time her laughter irritated me. I became suddenly conscious of my age. This brat is making fun of me! I looked at her severely and asked—Where do you live?

—Down there in that shanty colony, she said.

—So what are you doing up here so late in the evening?

I had expected her to irritate me by repeating her earlier answer, but she did not.

—I came up for a stroll, she said, and I wanted to see you.

I told myself to keep cool and get rid of her by giving her some change.

—What do you want from me? I asked.

—Nothing, she said.

I noticed we were walking side by side now, almost like father and daughter. The thought softened me. My boulder was unoccupied now. If this girl had not followed me, I would've gone very far today and returned home very late. I felt as if she had been sent after me to prevent me from going too far. I felt like telling her

An Evening with Bhookh Kumari

to rush back to her shanty colony and let me resume my long walk. But I didn't really want to resume it. My mood had changed. We were close to that boulder now. I stopped. She also stopped.

—What exactly were you doing here? I asked tenderly.

—I was waiting for you, she answered readily, I wanted to tell you something.

—Why don't you, then?

—I'll do that if you sit down with me on that boulder, she said.

The moment I sat down on that boulder with her, I felt like taking a plunge into that net of shanties glimmering far below. She sat right in front of me, reading me with her big luminous eyes. I hope she is not crazy. Bhookh Kumari! She must have given this name to herself. Her name gave me a salty sort of amusement. Her looks too. Her voice is like that of a princess in Indian movies. I'm sure she watches a lot of movies on TV. Every shanty has a colour TV. And a VCR. And a refrigerator. I checked myself. I am being uncharitable. Perhaps she sings as she begs. No, I can't imagine her begging.

Her knees were bruised. Her neck was so thin that even a child's hand could have encircled it. The luminosity of her eyes could be due to hunger. I felt like caressing her on her head, straightening the ribbon in her hair, and asking her when she had eaten last. She was gazing at me.

—Do you watch TV?

—Sometimes.

—Do you have one at home?

—No.

My question suddenly seemed vulgar to me—like the questions some writers put in the mouths of characters who go to a brothel only to talk to prostitutes. I decided I wouldn't ask her anything. I was curious about what she wanted to tell me. How does she know all about me? Does she know the problems I am facing these days? Poor dear Bhookh Kumari! Maybe she is a fairy from somewhere. I never saw a fairy even in my childhood, I won't see one now in my old age.

The evening had finally let her hair down. The sky was riddled with innumerable twinkling holes. The pale redness had faded out of the sky. I could hear the darkness vibrating. I sat there on that boulder like a lost old king listening to the fairy tales of the woodcutter's little daughter. The glow in Bhookh Kumari's eyes was undiminished. Her bare feet looked like two birds fast asleep.

—Say something, Bhookh Kumariji, I said.

—I'm waiting for the darkness to thicken; you can't be in a hurry to go back home, you are alone these days, aren't you?

This shook me up a bit. She's quite a spy.

—True, but I've to get back all the same, I said.

I felt like withdrawing my limp sentence. I also felt ashamed of myself for being so homebound.

—It's a little early for your evening ritual, she said.

Perhaps she knows the woman who cleans for me, I thought. All of a sudden I had an intense desire to accompany her to her shanty colony. But I decided not to tell her about it. That might scare her away. Besides, what would I do there? I can imagine everything—filth and all. My own place is surrounded by heaps of filth. Our country is great in this respect. You are not too far from filth, no matter where you live, in the so-called posh areas or the shanty colonies.

—Yes, it's a little early for my evening addiction, I said, but I do skip it for a day or so every now and then.

—Really! she said

—By God! I said in English.

We broke into simultaneous laughter.

—Your laughter is nice, she said after a short pause.

I wasn't prepared for this compliment. I couldn't tell what was on her mind. Perhaps I should have said something but I didn't.

—So you sit here on this boulder every evening and look down at the shanties glimmering far below, she said.

I waited for her to add that she knew I thought of taking a plunge into that network of glimmering shanties, but she didn't add anything.

—Can you see this boulder from your shanty? I asked her.

There was a long pause before she opened her mouth. When she did, her voice was full of mischief—I can see the whole world from my shanty.

An Evening with Bhookh Kumari

I don't know why I was shaken on hearing this. I guess I was not prepared for this flight of her fancy.

—But why didn't you stop here today? she asked.

—Because my place was not vacant, I said.

—So you saw me? she asked

—I didn't see you, but I saw that my place was occupied, I answered.

—But it wasn't, she said, for I was sitting where I am sitting now, and *this* is not your place.

—I consider the whole boulder as my place, I rejoined. I had thought she would either laugh, or say something at which I would, but she seemed lost in some other thought.

That was the first time I had sat on that boulder with a smart little stranger. What is it that she wants to tell me? Why is she hesitating? I should make it easy for her, say something to draw her out. Perhaps someone in her family is sick. She needs my help. Perhaps she is just a clever little crook. I smelled meanness in my speculations and said, by way of diverting my attention—Do you go to school?

—I used to, but not any more, she said.

—Why did you stop?

—I didn't like it there.

—But why?

—I already knew what they wanted to teach me; I'm pretty sharp, she said with such a straight face that I couldn't help laughing. She did not laugh with me.

—Don't you believe? she asked.

So she is aware of even this flaw in my character! I got a hold of myself and said—Don't I believe in what?

I was afraid she'd retort: In anything? But she spared me that and said—In my sharpness?

—Of course, I do . . . .

She interrupted me and said—But you are surprised?

The effect she had produced on me could not be expressed by 'surprised' but I had no desire to argue with her. So I kept quiet. I had started enjoying her words and actions the way an old depressed character of a novel would enjoy the words and actions of a lively young character of raw age and ripe intelligence. I felt like inviting her to come and see me every evening on the same spot. I didn't do it. Somehow it didn't seem right. I was afraid of scaring her away. I was afraid she would say something that would turn me off. I made up my mind to talk less and listen more, for any wrong move or word could very well destroy the fragile harmony of our encounter. Excessive caution would, on the other hand, affect my own tenuous spontaneity. I was in a fix, but she sat pretty in front of me like a princess. Bhookh Kumari! I was sure her parents had little to do with that name. I thought of asking her about her parents but then the inquiry seemed improper. The darkness had thickened by now. A thin fingernail of the moon adorned the sky. Bhookh Kumari's big eyes had become even more luminous. Only undernourished children have such huge beautiful eyes. Her wrists seemed to be made of black glass but her feet were like two healthy birds.

I was disturbed in my reverie by her next question—The story you are struggling with these days ... how's that going?

—Not well, I answered noncommittally.

Perhaps she was about to tell me what she wanted to.

—I know, she said.

—What! I exclaimed.

—That your story is not going well.

—But how do you know that? I wondered.

—I'm a rag-picker, you see; I work the rubbish heaps, and the one at the back of your bungalow is in my beat, she informed me.

I was overwhelmed.

—So apart from knowing how your story is going, I also know how you yourself are, she told me.

—How's that? I asked in a feeble voice.

—From the empty bottles you throw away, she answered.

I laughed nervously, like a person overwhelmed by a prodigy. For a while my laughter disturbed the thick darkness, then it died.

—So, then, how am I doing these days? I asked her.

—Not well at all: in fact, you are stuck, which is why I've come to see you, she said blithely.

—But why here? Why didn't you come to see me at my place?

An Evening with Bhookh Kumari

I'm always in, as you probably know, I said.

—I do, but if I'd sought you out there, you might have taken me for a beggar; you wouldn't have talked to me properly; you wouldn't have offered me a seat; you'd have considered me filthy; you'd have suspected my motives; but here in the dark we sit face to face on this boulder like equals; of course, I'm so very junior to you in age, almost like one of your daughters or even granddaughters, but here you can't intimidate me. And besides, over there, your tail-less dog Gogo would've made it impossible for us to talk. He goes wild, as you don't know, as soon as he sniffs me out; I can't do my picking in peace when he is around; your shredded waste paper, especially, he guards like a lion; I can get at it only at night....

She was talking about rag-picking and rubbish heaps and Gogo but it seemed to me as if she was telling me fairy tales. I wanted to lie down on that boulder and close my eyes and ask her to go on and on about rubbish heaps. I wondered why I had never spotted her on the rubbish heap at the back of my bungalow. I walk by that heap at least twice a day, glancing at the rag-pickers, tugging at Gogo, ordering him to calm down, smelling the filth, prodding my blocked story, my blocked life. When Gogo pushes the backdoor open and runs out of the house, I run after him, thinking that people in the lane would be wondering about the mysterious sources of my energy and my crazy fondness for Gogo. Every time I see that rubbish heap, I think of it as a heap of discarded reality. Bhookh Kumari must have seen me many times. I too must have seen her, but then why didn't I recognize her here? How could I not notice a girl like her: a red ribbon in her hair, a glow in her big eyes, and the bearing of a princess of the rubbish heaps! I felt ashamed and angry at my lack of perception. I wanted to apologize to her.

—You see, she went on, I could've talked to you about these things only in the dark, here, looking at you while you are looking at those shanties far below and playing with the idea of taking a plunge....

She would've gone on but I interrupted her with an exclamation I can't describe, which must have struck her as being

161

ridiculous, for she burst out laughing.

—Why are you so incredulous? she asked, can't I guess what you think as you sit brooding on this boulder? I told you I am very sharp. I have imagination. True, you are a writer while I am not, but that does not mean I can't imagine; you see, I too have often thought of taking the plunge that you think about. It may well be that there's something in this boulder or perhaps those shanties that tempts one to take a plunge....

I gazed at her in silence. She was really marvellous. She did know everything about me. I could detect that she was parodying my train of thought and tone of speech. And she is a rag-picker! Bhookh Kumari! Her big eyes glittered like stars in the dark. I wanted to touch those eyes. By now I was convinced she wouldn't be scared by anything I said or did. By now I was convinced she was extraordinary. Extraordinariness is not confined to any one class. Or perhaps she was a fairy princess after all. She had unbalanced me.

—Are you a rag-picker, really? I asked her.

—Of course, I am. What else can I be? I'm poor and uneducated. I'm lucky I belong to a family of rag-pickers. I could've been named *Ghoora Bai* also. My mother was known by this name. Rag-picking is foul work, but it isn't difficult. Besides, I'm quite an expert rag-picker; I may well be the best in town. I can tell at a glance what is worth picking and what is not. Of course, I don't pick rags only. Unlike others of my trade, I don't have to thrash about in the rubbish with my hands and feet. And then sometimes I find such wonderful things. Our shanty is a little museum of wonderful things. I've never been short of toys. Nor of clothes. Nor of food, in fact. The things people throw away! I picked this dress and this ribbon from your rubbish heap. Don't stare at my feet; I keep them bare by choice. I have a fairly large assortment of shoes, but don't see any fun in wandering unless my feet are occasionally quickened by a thorn or a pebble. People have acquired heaps of black money; that's why the rubbish heaps are rich. My mother used to bless the municipality for not removing rubbish regularly. My mother collected quite a dowry for me entirely from the rubbish heaps. You see, we rag-pickers have a world of our own. You need not pity us. People have made millions out of us rag-pickers. Well, I look upon my work as a form of art. You write, I pick rubbish heaps. The very thought makes my mouth salivate. I can see you are feeling sick.

I wasn't feeling sick but I *was* on the verge of tears. I wanted to stop her mouth with my hand. An extraordinary girl like her has to eat people's leavings! I was on the verge of tears born of shame and rage and impotence. I was overwhelmed by the utter obscenity of my writing and way of life. But I couldn't lose sight of this hard fact: that I wouldn't be able to do a thing for that fairy princess of a little girl. I wanted to get up and run off to my bungalow.

Bhookh Kumari must have seen through my dilemma, for she said—Well, I told you all this because you expected me to; perhaps I've told you far too much; but you should be tough; you are a writer, and a writer should have a strong stomach; he should be able to take in everything. Moreover, you have that great rubbish heap at the back of your bungalow where you must have seen filth of every kind. I'm sure you have seen me there too; I see you all the time, running after your Gogo or standing over that bent old woman, eating garbage or ogling that beautiful tribal woman. You should be proud of your rubbish heap; it is full of delightful surprises, the best of them being your waste paper, crumpled into balls; I take them home and have fun unravelling them and piecing them together; some of them are totally blank; others are untorn; I like those best, for I can smoothe them out and read what you have written; quite often it is the same sentence repeated several times; I find it very funny; sometimes it is nothing more than nonsensical combinations of letters or words. Now you know how I know that neither you nor your story is doing well these days—your working title for your story seems to be 'Hunger', isn't it?

I didn't give myself time to feel surprised or pleased at the care she took in collecting my crumpled and shredded waste paper; I just let myself go, without censoring what came to my lips.

—I don't believe you are a rag-picker, I blurted out, I don't believe you live in that shanty colony; I don't believe you eat garbage; I don't believe you collect my waste paper and piece or paste it together in order to read what I write; I don't believe you are sitting there in front of me; your language, your style, your sharpness, your irony, your manners, your voice, your self-confidence, your laughter, your eyes, where would a poor rag-picking girl pick up all this? From my waste paper? I don't believe it. Tell me the truth. Who are you?

I was trembling; so was my voice. Till then I had taken everything as a sort of joke. No, not as a joke but as something essentially plausible. No, not even that, but something I could still take with a mixture of curiosity and scepticism and amusement. But her casual talk of eating garbage and collecting my waste paper had thrown me off balance.

She took my hands in hers. My trembling soft hands seemed to be panting like two wounded birds in her stable coarse ones.

—*Arre*! You shouldn't go on like this, she admonished me, if you can't believe, you can't; but don't take it personally; why be so emotional! You are a man of experience and a writer; you have travelled all over the world, seen all sorts of strange people; you must have seen all sorts of marvels in your dreams, if not in real life. Nothing should throw you off balance. Don't believe anything; but why fly into this state of fury, and that too over me, poor me, poor Bhookh Kumari! All right, you are free to call me Bhookh Ki Mari! Come on, now, let's have a smile. Take a long breath. Once more. There! You are not trembling any more. An artist ought to be a magician. He should make marvels, not disbelieve them. I know you are alone these days; and you are working too hard; and you are not eating well; and you are drinking too much; and, on top of it, you have writer's block; I can well imagine your frustration, but I can help you; in fact, I am here this evening only to do that, you see . . . .

She went on in that vein for quite some time while I regretted my outburst quietly. Her words had a magical effect on me, though; so did the gentle pressure of her hands. I felt she was trying to dispel my disbelief with her magic. I was drawing strength from her words and hands. I had a great desire to ask her to join me in taking a plunge into that network of glimmering shanties far below. I was regaining my composure gradually but my essential disbelief was still unshaken. I told myself to relax and soak up what

An Evening with Bhookh Kumari

she was saying instead of resisting it. Soon enough I was my normal sane self.

—I shouldn't have lost self-control, I said.

—Never mind, she said.

She let go of my hands. The beautiful coarseness of her small hands had permeated my big flabby ones. Neither of us spoke for a while. I kept peering into her big bright eyes, she into my small dim ones.

—But don't you believe? she asked finally.

I wasn't prepared for that question. Earlier, when she had raised the same question, out of consideration for me, she had given it a narrow meaning; this time she had left it wide open. An answer to that question would have involved me in an examination of my entire life. So I kept quiet. She did not press her question.

—How old are you? I asked, primarily to take my attention away from the thought that I might have extinguished the magic of the evening by my disbelief.

—About twelve or thirteen, and you?

—About sixty or sixty-one, I said.

—You can walk like a sixteen-year-old when you want to, she remarked.

I smiled even as I felt flattered. So she even knows my sensitivity about my age.

—Now, if you promise that you won't fly into a rage, I'd like to say what I want to.

—I promise, I said solemnly.

—Tell me, then, why that story of yours, 'Hunger', is causing you so much difficulty; why doesn't it move? She looked very concerned as she said this.

I wasn't prepared for her question. I thought of putting her off by saying that every story had always caused me difficulty, that difficulty was the price one paid for the delight of finishing a story, that every artist had his problems, and similar other unconvincing clichés. But I couldn't possibly do that to Bhookh Kumari. So I said—I don't quite know why; I don't want to talk about it either; I'm afraid I'll kill the desire to write that story if I do, and then you won't find those crumpled balls of waste paper on that heap.

—Don't talk about it then, she said—I've gotten addicted to smoothing those crumpled balls of paper and putting them together into readable stuff; I've a whole heap of them in my shanty; my mother would've burnt them.

—What happened to your mother?

—She died.

—Of what?

—Of cholera.

I didn't have the heart to ask her about her father. But she seemed to have divined my curiosity.

—I don't have a father. I mean I don't know who he was or is; my mother never told me about him; people of my colony called me a bastard; I used to swear and throw stones at them, which provoked them into torturing me even more. Of late, I've stopped minding them. One night my mother came to me in a dream and advised me not to mind. It was good advice, for people have stopped torturing me now. It doesn't give them any pleasure any more to call me a bastard since I've stopped flaring up and hitting back. People would do anything for pleasure.

Her last sentence was full of the wisdom of the world.

—I too am fond of writing, she told me cheerfully.

I wasn't surprised but I kept quiet.

—You must be thinking who isn't, she said.

I wasn't thinking that. I couldn't tell what I was thinking about. In order to get out of the darkness of my thoughts I said—What do you write?

—Nothing. I'm just fond of it. For now I'm just busy collecting paper and experience.

Her 'experience' twinkled like a magical glow-worm in the darkness of my thoughts. She looked like a prodigy making good-natured fun of herself and me. I brightened up a little. I told myself I'd take her home with me for dinner, I'd ask her to wash her hands first, I might even ask her to take a quick bath, I'd give her a shirt and pair of trousers and have her old clothes thrown on the heap, I'd let her keep the red ribbon; she would emerge like a flower from under her dirt; perhaps I'd have her admitted into a good school . . . .

An Evening with Bhookh Kumari

I'd strayed far in my fantasy and was a little embarrassed by its romantic colour. I feared that Bhookh Kumari would divine my mind and say: What a wild imagination! But instead she said in a mysteriously mature voice—You won't believe it, but I can really help you out of your block.

I gave a start. My fantasy disappeared. Bhookh Kumari was waiting for my response to her offer of help.

—Forget about my disbelief; I accept your offer of help, I said.

Bhookh Kumari got up and stood erect on the boulder. She straightened her blue dress, yawned, and said with a smile—Well, then, you'll have to come over to my shanty colony and stay there with me for a few days; of course, you'll have to take off these fancy clothes and wear some rags I'll give you; you'll sleep by the side of an open drain and put your bungalow and bathrooms out of your mind; you'll have to go back to the days of your youth when you knew hunger from personal experience and dreamt of abolishing it; you'll have to eat the leavings of other people; you'll have to overcome your nausea. . . .

She went on like that for a while longer as I listened to her intently, my head down like that of a devotee. Her voice seemed to be descending from the high heavens. I couldn't get up the nerve to say that her conditions were acceptable to me.

Then she stopped her outpour abruptly. I raised my head. She smiled. She had seen through my hesitation.

—You don't have to decide right now, she said, I shall come to you in your dreams one of these nights; till then you should let my conditions sink into your mind.

She jumped off the boulder and started running down the slope toward her shanty colony glimmering far below. I sat there for a while, looking at her receding figure, then got up and started walking wearily back to my bungalow.

Many days have gone by. Every night I wait for the dream in which Bhookh Kumari will appear to me again and I give her my answer.

The Old Man in the Park

I

I am a stranger in this neighbourhood. I came here recently, after having tried several other neighbourhoods. I am face to face with the same old problems. When I get sick of them, I get up and go for a stroll. I set out even if it is midnight or fierce noon. There is nobody here to stop or nag me. I am not afraid of being robbed of my wallet or watch, or of being beaten or killed or kidnapped by someone who will then demand a fat ransom from my sons. I have no sons. I am not afraid of losing my balance in the dark or my mind in the fierce sun. I am not worried that somebody's dog will bite me or a policeman take me in for vagabondage. I do not fear that someone will take me for a thief or an assassin and call the police. I do occasionally get upset by one fear—that someone will take pity on me and insist on helping me. Until this day no one has, even though I look pitiable enough. I cannot turn to look around, keep my back straight, or talk audibly. While walking I look like a large insect aping a small old man. But I have noticed that nobody takes pity on those who look pitiable. They often feel contempt and

The Old Man in the Park

revulsion and pass these off as pity. Even so, I cannot quite shake off this fear. I am always on my guard during my strolls. I keep turning to look around, I keep my back straight, I try to be audible even if all this effort is extremely painful and pointless. Perhaps I look even more pitiable and ridiculous because of all these pointless efforts. But then I am indifferent to what others think about me. I know there is a contradiction there but I shall let it be. I get a lot of satisfaction from my effort to keep my metaphorical chin up. My ego remains erect, and I am beguiled by the delusion of my self-sufficiency. I am sure people notice me in the park, if nowhere else. Those who are worse off than me draw inspiration from me; those who are better off bless their better stars; those who are absolutely well off, I mean incomparably well off, tell themselves: There, but for the grace of God, go I. In short, I have this cold comfort that even in my pitiable state I cannot help performing a useful social function. But the terrible truth of the matter is that I draw no comfort, cold or warm, from any self-deluding thought. Most of the time I am either harassed by my trivial worldly and bodily problems or by those huge questions that will always remain unanswered by me: Why was I born? Why am I alive? Why don't I die? Where will I go after death?

Ever since I came to this neighbourhood, these huge questions have become even more obsessive. Perhaps this neighbourhood is my last stop. On some midnights and fierce noons, when I am slouching around like a self-respecting two-legged insect, a shadow appears and starts slouching along with me, whispering incoherently to me about those huge questions. I think that shadow is my only true companion now.

II

I have been seeing him for the past several days in the park, morning and evening, sitting disconsolately on that decrepit bench. Every day I detect a new similarity between himself and me. Every day he scares me a little more than the previous day. I cannot say whether he too detects a new similarity between me and himself every day, whether I too scare him a little more than the previous day. I do not know whether he is even aware of me the way I am of him.

Every morning when I set foot in that park, I find him sitting on that bench in a posture that suggests someone else has put him there, that he is an extension of that bench, that he too is made of concrete like that bench. I see crows and pigeons frisking all around him. There is no one else in the park at that time. I cannot imagine the preoccupations of his mind. Oblivious of the crows and pigeons around, he sits there in a posture that suggests to me that someone has put him there and disappeared. I do not think he is a beggar but like every lost old man he looks beggarly enough. I do not think he is homeless, but like every old man, sitting by himself in a deserted park, he looks homeless enough. I do not think he is crazy, but like every abandoned old man he looks crazy enough. Had he a beard and long hair, I would have taken him for an eccentric. He appears to be eccentric not because of his dress or appearance, but because of his utter motionlessness, and also because of those crows and pigeons. It is quite likely he throws some food to them but I have never seen him doing that. Perhaps the birds shit on him. I do not think he ever wipes the shit off.

I have begun to be worried about the ever-new similarities that I see between him and me. I have a fear these similarities will become an obsession and drive me into spying on him. I have a fear he will soon start stalking my dreams, he will change them into nightmares and me into a ghost. I have a fear he will vanish one of these days and I shall not be able to get rid of him forever. I shall think it is I who scared him away by staring at him, by thinking about him intensely, by imagining similarities between himself and me, by putting my telepathic pressure on him. I shall regret not having made friends with him, not having heard from him his life story, not having told him mine, not having told him about those similarities between himself and me. On trying to recall him, I shall not see his face clearly. Then I shall wonder whether I saw him at all, except in my nightmares. When these anxieties become unbearable, I feel like walking over to him, sitting down with him, and start pouring my heart out to him. But I am a prisoner of my inhibitions. I shall never have the courage to approach him, offer him my hand and ask who he is, what he broods about sitting there, how he spends the rest of his day, what spell he casts on those crows and pigeons, where he sleeps at night, why I detect a new similarity between himself and me every day. I envy as well as abominate those people who can pose such unambiguous questions to anyone who looks like them. No, I will not do anything of the sort. As long as he is there, I shall keep thinking about him. I shall do nothing more than that.

III

Today my dusty green bench in the park was occupied by a beaten old man, whom I sometimes see trampling the withered grass listlessly when I take my evening stroll. Before today I never dared to go near him. When he is trampling the withered grass of the park, his head lolls in a way that makes me think his neck is broken, that someone has broken it. He himself gives the impression that he is groping in the grass with his feet for something he does not really need or hope to find, but would perhaps not mind keeping if he found it. I cast a casual eye on him whenever he is there but I doubt if he ever saw me before today. He is always alone and self-absorbed, like me. But, then, even I do look around off and on as I walk. Sometimes I stamp my feet to scare a crow or pigeon away; sometimes I mutter endearments to a baby or dog; sometimes I shoo a pig away. But he hardly ever lifts his eyes from the withered grass. I imagine one would have to lie down on the grass underneath his eyes to catch his attention.

When he is trampling the withered grass, there is no one else in the park except me and a rather colourful bunch of dark pale nannies on a mound in the middle of the park, taking bad care of well-turned-out toddlers and dogs. I watch those nannies from a decent distance. They are young and aggressive. My desire to have a close look at them is killed by the fear that one of them will burst into derisory laughter that may induce the rest of them to join in, and then the toddlers too may start laughing, which in turn may rouse the dogs into a choral bark and the birds into cawing and twittering. I do not want to create this pandemonium. I am not one of those dignified old people at whom no nanny, howsoever young and aggressive, would ever dare to laugh.

I do not know what kind of an old man my friend the grass-trampler is. Perhaps he is one of those who are always busy seeking something they don't really need or hope to find, but are still mildly interested in finding. In any case, today he sat on my dusty green bench instead of doing his usual thing. His neck looked broken as usual. The nannies and the toddlers and the dogs had gone home. Perhaps I had reached the park later than usual or the others had left it earlier than usual. So I made a beeline of sorts to the dusty green bench. I do not make a beeline to it every time I enter the park. I do not go to that park every day. There are three parks in my neighbourhood. So I keep changing the venue of my strolls so as to prevent them from falling into a rut. It is a different misery that, in spite of this precaution, my strolls and I are gradually falling into a rut. Well, then, today, when I reached my bench, I found him sitting there. I was surprised. Had I noticed him in time I would have changed the direction of my beeline of sorts. But when I saw him, I was hardly two or three small steps away from the bench. He must have heard the whisper of my feet. It did not seem proper to retrace my steps. I did not wish to offend him. He could have raised his lolling head and taunted: Look here, brother, why are you running away from me; I am not a leper, am I? No, he would not have said anything of the sort. No one but me can even think of such a thing, not to mention say it. Well, for whatever reason, I kept going toward the bench. He did not raise his lolling head. Just as I was about to lower myself on the bench, he moved aside. I whispered my thanks. He did not say anything. I was prepared for a long burdensome silence, even for his abrupt departure, but not for what actually happened. A couple of minutes after I had parked myself, he started speaking in a thick blank voice, like an aged child reciting a lesson he had learnt by rote—I've been unsuccessful in everything I've done. I've been unsuccessful in my own eyes as well as in others'. I haven't achieved anything. I have lost this world as well as the next. I am neither here nor there. I lack the warmth of faith. I lack the light of vision. I am a zero. But I am alive. Why am I? My self-knowledge is killing me. But I am alive. Why am I? I am a zero. In my own eyes as well as in others'. I am . . . .

For some time I sat there, stunned, listening to his un-self-pitying monotone. Then something happened to me and I started chanting monotonously, along with him: I've been unsuccessful in everything I've done. I've been unsuccessful in my own eyes as well as . . . .

Had a third person been watching or overhearing us, he would have taken us for two old twins chanting a mantra in monotone.

IV

Today I was just about to complete my first round in the park when a beautiful old woman got up from a green bench under a neem tree and started walking with me. I felt a little unsettled at first but recovered soon enough. It is a public park, and if a beautiful old woman decides to join a gentlemanly old stroller, it should not surprise or unsettle him. I myself would not be capable of any such spontaneous action. I looked askance at my companion. She looked straight at me and smiled. Her smile was transparent and light. I could not quite smile back but my lips did crack open a bit. My pace had become a little brisk because of her. Had a third person been observing us, she would not have guessed we were utter strangers, that I had never even seen her before, that I was enjoying her company as a gift of the gods. We completed one round in silence. During the second I asked her without looking at her: What is the secret of your beauty? She answered without a moment's hesitation: I never had any expectation from anybody, not even from myself; so I never felt disappointed or disillusioned; what you take for beauty is perhaps nothing but the absence of expectations and yearnings; it has nothing to do with my physical features. I should have touched her feet and kissed her hands but I started shivering instead. She asked: Why have you started shivering? I answered: Because of how you look and what you said just now;

I've never before seen or heard anyone like you. At this we laughed together. Her laughter was profound, mine hollow. After the third round we stopped near the park gate. She told me that was her first time in that park and would also be her last. I did not ask her why it would be her last time. We smiled at each other and went our separate ways. Her smile was beautiful, mine grateful.

V

I have returned to this my pitiless city after years of knocking about, like a handful of dust, for the last time, I hope. I have returned, clutching to my bosom the desire to die here, looking like a bedraggled effigy made of dried-up longings or perhaps like some dream of a madman.

Years ago I started my journey from here, along with some fellow-travellers, some of whom are perhaps still around, suffering somewhere. I have no contact with any of them now. They visit me only in my memories and nightmares now, and that too infrequently. The desire to meet them has died but not the fear that I will run into one or several of them one of these days. I am sure they too spend their mornings and evenings in some pale narrow park on the pretext of taking a stroll—shuffling their feet, self-lost, seeing their ghostly past in every other old man, regrets incarnate.

I can still see the sun and dust of that distant past scattered all around me. In those days I myself used to flit about like dust and sunshine in some select neighbourhoods of this city, for fun as well as work. In those days we were dedicated to the task of obliterating the distinction between work and fun. Our vain efforts gave rise to many a dark blue folly. I often think that but for those follies we could not have survived the dread of those days.

Dread used to be our favourite word then. Also our favourite experience. Some select neighbourhoods of this city—chief among them was one called Fatehpuri—used to yield us a dread of an exceptional intensity. So I used to haunt them like a wild ghost and return to my pad late in the night loaded with dread of an exceptional intensity. I used to change my pad so often that some smart alecs called me a no-good nomad. Every pad looked more desolate than the previous one. But I felt at home in desolation. These days my memory is often lit up by the beauty of some of my desolate pads—like ruins sometimes are by glow-worms.

Now, of course, I lack the energy as well as the will to flit about like dust and sun in any neighbourhood. Besides, the city has changed into a gigantic monster. My favourite neighbourhoods have been swallowed by this monster. Now I lack the courage to explore them for dread. Now I am reduced to taking listless strolls in a pale narrow park of this alien neighbourhood, sifting my dusty memories, counting my few blessings, accepting in the glow of a luminous moment everything and nothing, rejecting in the glow of another luminous moment everything and nothing.

This morning, I was taking my stroll when I was seized by a feeling that someone hidden somewhere was staring at me. I do not get such seizures very often, but, whenever I do, my body begins to reverberate with a resounding stillness. These seizures happen suddenly. When I am locked in my void-room, I overcome the reverberation caused by them, search every nook and corner, but am unable to find the source of the gaze. When I am wandering about in my nightmareland, I get up with a start as if I have been pierced by an arrow; then I spend the whole night searching my whole house and my whole past but do not find the source of that gaze. At last I collapse to the conclusion that, even though I am an agnostic, I am not quite free of the spell of the invisible forces, and the source of that gaze is in those very invisible forces.

This morning also, at first I thought those invisible forces were glaring at me. I raised my head and looked around. All I saw were a few stunted trees, a few self-absorbed pigeons, a few dark nannies, two dogs, five toddlers, one bull, two pigs, a few butterflies, and several knock-kneed old folks doing their horrifying calisthenics. I failed to find the source of the gaze. I was about to lower my head and resume my listless stroll when I noticed an old man leaning against the boundary wall of the park. His eyes were like two wide open tiny windows. Strangers with unblinking eyes strike me with an unbearable terror. The unblinking eyes of that old man too would have affected me similarly but for the fact that I had recognized him.

I walked over to him, taking small steps. His face was like a piece of wrinkled wood lit by moonlight. The light came from his eyes, which even in his youth days was the sole support of his rather ordinary face. Even in his youth he looked elderly. His voice had the sound of wood. His forehead was always overcast by fundamental questions. A meeting with him used to produce in me the same exceptionally intense dread that a romp in some selected areas of the city used to.

Today we met after about forty years. My face was cracked by a confused smile as soon as I recognized him, but I saw no crack in his. When I offered him my hand, he placed a limp leaf-like hand in mine. I did not press it much.

—I was informed by someone that you had returned from abroad and your abode is now in this neighbourhood.

His voice was formal and wooden. I kept quiet. I was afraid my voice would remind him of an owl's.

—My abode is also in this neighbourhood now.

Rather than being surprised I was reinforced in my apprehension that several of my old companions were living their last days out all around me, and all of them would keep running into me and after a few weeks I would be surrounded by people as far gone as me; they would share their miseries with me and expect me to reciprocate; they would complain about their daughters-in-law and wives; they would flaunt their philosophies before me and expect me to be impressed; they would talk about their diseases and drugs and envy me when they found out I had no problem other than ennui and disbelief. It is because of these fears that I always keep my head down during my strolls and also keep changing my routes and venues. I never look any old man or woman in the eye. Whenever I see the pale moon of recognition rising on some strange old face, I turn around abruptly and break into a run. Well, breaking into a run is not that easy for me now, but I try to move away as fast as I can.

I avoid my old comrades not because I consider myself either superior or inferior to them but because I am afraid of recognizing all my ghosts in them. But if this is true, why did I go over to him today instead of running away after I had recognized him? Perhaps only because I had taken his gaze, before I had seen it, for that of invisible forces. I gave him the benefit of my error.

So I stood next to my friend of the wooden voice, thinking that even in those days he used the formal 'you' for me. The wooden fence of formality he had raised between himself and me was still intact. I had this consolation that he would neither tell nor ask me about anything personal. I was hoping we would part company after a few more moments of formal silence—he would express the hope we'd meet again and I'd do the same. But he startled me by saying—If you have some spare time, I'd like to have the pleasure of your company at my abode, which is not too far from here, over a cup of tea; we could then exchange our views about so many grave issues the country is facing.

Even in those days he used to be fond of exchanging views on grave issues. He used to refer to a great thinker in every third sentence. One felt that a log of wood was uttering an irrefutable, but unnecessary, truth.

His 'abode' was a single room. He had fixed one corner for cooking, another for bathing and washing, still another for three overladen rickety book-racks. The rest of the room was for everything else—sitting, sleeping, reading, writing, and, of course, exchange of views on grave issues. The walls were blank, the floor bare. The windows had unfitting curtains. Everything in the room was plunged in deep thought. I had a feeling that every now and then those things broke their silence and asked one another—Have you arrived at any conclusion to any fundamental question?

I did not see any photograph of a woman or child in the room. There was no stain of domesticity anywhere. It seemed my friend had brought me to the room he used to live in forty years ago. It seemed he had been moving about with that room on his shoulders and had finally put it down in that neighbourhood.

While he was preparing tea, I started roaming, with my eyes closed, all those neighbourhoods of this pitiless city which used to produce in me a dread beyond hope or despair—Pulbangash, Majnoon Ka Teela, Sitaram Bazar, Turkman Gate, Todar Mal Lane, Anand Parbat, Mata Sundari Road, Andha Mughal, Dareeba

Kalan, Gali Naiwalan, Guston Buston Road and, beyond and above all these, FATEHPURI!

VI

Sometimes, for my evening stroll, I take a path where I am sure I will not run into anyone. I do not hear any sound except the shuffle of my feet and my wheezing. My mind goes absolutely empty as soon as I set foot on that path. Sometimes, however, a beautiful old woman appears from nowhere and starts walking along with me like my shadow. I have never seen her appearing. I have never even looked at her but I am convinced she is beautiful. We have never exchanged a word or touch. I have an impression her mind too is empty when she is with me. During the stroll I am aware of her without thinking of her. I have a feeling she is an avatar of the old woman who joined me in the park one evening and told me the secret of her beauty. When I am about to end my stroll, she disappears. I have seen her disappearing. I am afraid the old woman in the park was imaginary even as this one is. I do not quite believe this though. I have a feeling I am busy creating a beautiful old woman who will take on a form and name one of these evenings.

VII

A few nights back I saw a luminous old man in one of my dreams. He had a red beard that looked like a flame. His eyes seemed to connect the exterior with the interior. I was taking a stroll in the dream. I saw the luminous old man standing on the mound in the middle of the park. The distance between us was great but it seemed short. I took him for a shepherd at first. Then the park changed into an ocean. Now it appeared as if the luminous old man and his mound had emerged from that ocean. I thought he might be the statue of a Greek god. He had a gnarled staff in his right hand, a flower in his left. That made me think he might be a prophet. I found myself standing beside him—like a small old man standing at the feet of a tall old man. I stood with my head bent. I was ready for his staff as well as his flower. I had my eyes closed. I heard a roar that could have come from the old man or the ocean. I did not open my eyes. And I thought that that was the sound of his staff. Then I heard absolute silence. And I thought that that was the sound of his flower. After some time, when I opened my eyes, I found myself all ready for my morning stroll, my body light, my mind empty.

VIII

It appeared from their numbers and expressions that all the old-timers of the city were about to go out in a silent funereal procession. I appeared to be part of the crowd as well as apart from it, watching it from a little mound, having my fun. I appeared to be young as well as old, known as well as unknown to the rest of the crowd. There was no breeze in the park. There were no birds. The sky had changed into a mountain of dust. The light was such that I could not tell whether it was day or night. I wondered if they had broadcast or telecast an announcement I had missed. It could be that the gathering was the result of some collective dream all of us had had. Then I started imagining that the gathering was a prelude to a protest march against the indifference of the authorities toward old folks. Some demands flashed across my mind: rejuvenate the parks of the city; rid them of the trees and plants and people we are allergic to; put some birds in them, whose twitterings can lull us into a false peace; we want heavenly music in the parks. Then I wondered if we had gathered to mourn the loss of a veteran stroller who had stuck to his routine unto the last. Then I decided it was our last stroll. This conjecture made me happy beyond words. My happiness drove all other conjectures out of my mind. I walked over to a friendly looking tree on the mound and stood under it, a little above the other strollers, like a general about to view a march past. Suddenly they started marching past me, their heads turned towards me, doing their heart-rending best to keep their warped bodies straight, smiling feebly at some black joke of their own devising. I felt like shouting: Stop smiling and be done! Then I thought I would not have the right roar in my voice. Then I also started smiling feebly.

After, I cannot tell how long, all of us faded out; I last of all.

MORE ABOUT PENGUINS

For further information about books available from Penguins in India write to Penguin Books (India) Ltd, B4/246, Safdarjung Enclave, New Delhi 110 029.

In the UK: For a complete list of books available from Penguins in the United Kingdom write to Dept. EP, Penguin Books Ltd, Harmondsworth, Middlesex UB7 0DA.

In the U.S.A.: For a complete list of books available from Penguins in the United States write to Dept. DG, Penguin Books, 299 Murray Hill Parkway, East Rutherford, New Jersey 07073.

In Canada: For a complete list of books available from Penguins in Canada write to Penguin Books Canada Ltd, 2801 John Street, Markham, Ontario L3R 1B4.

In Australia: For a complete list of books available from Penguins in Australia write to the Marketing Department, Penguin Books Australia Ltd, P.O. Box 257, Ringwood, Victoria 3134.

In New Zealand: For a complete list of books available from Penguins in New Zealand write to the Marketing Department, Penguin Books (N.Z.) Ltd, Private Bag, Takapuna, Auckland 9.

FOR THE BEST IN PAPERBACKS, LOOK FOR THE 🐧

KINGDOM'S END AND OTHER STORIES
Saadat Hasan Manto
Translated by Khalid Hasan

The stories in this collection, which are a selection from Manto's best work, can be separated into three categories—those dealing with the low life in Bombay and the Punjab, amongst prostitutes and their clients, pimps, and madams, set amongst the streets and cheap bars of Indian cities, and those about the Partition massacres of 1947. The third category satirizes the corruption and hypocrisy of priests for whom Manto had a particular loathing. A writer who will provoke concern, debate and introspection as well as delight with his brilliant story-telling.

"The undisputed master of the modern Indian short story" —*Salman Rushdie*

FOR THE BEST IN PAPERBACKS, LOOK FOR THE 🐧

FAIR TREE OF THE VOID

Vilas Sarang
Translated from the Marathi by the author and
Breon Mitchell

In a startling blend of the real and the fantastic, these stories create a world populated wholly by solitaries—usually lonely single males who lead sterile, aimless lives. As a function of their passivity, these characters often find themselves drawn into extraordinary situations where the bizarre is commonplace: one protagonist is cast ashore on an island where there are only half women, another metamorphoses into a giant penis, a third is witness to idols of gods in a festival procession coming alive and disappearing into the streets of Bombay.... Sarang's world, then, is one that is poised between the provinces of imagination and reality—and the obvious influences are the great masters of this form of literature—Kafka, Camus, Beckett and Borges. Yet, Sarang's voice is unique in that he transcends those who have gone before to emerge in a place that we have never visited, the true hallmark of a writer of genius.

FOR THE BEST IN PAPERBACKS, LOOK FOR THE 🐧

DELIVERANCE AND OTHER STORIES
Premchand

Translated from the Hindi by David Rubin

Premchand was an extraordinarily versatile writer who first began publishing around the turn of the century. Equally at home in Urdu and in Hindi, he wrote some fourteen novels, three hundred short stories and several hundred essays. Although he was influenced by Tolstoy, Maupassant and Chekov, his strength was his ability to capture village and small town India in minute and glittering detail. This collection brings together the finest stories Premchand wrote—including classics such as *The Chess Players, The Shroud, Deliverance* and the wonderfully comic Moteram Shastri Stories.

'Probably the greatest figure in modern Indian literature.'
—*The Scotsman*